PILLAGE

Family Tree

Hermitage (Scotland, 1751) —m— Hope

Lucinda —m— Edward Iris Naomi

Olivia Rose Bruno —m— Catharine

Diana —m— Daniel Annabelle

Taft —m— Esmerelda

Morgan —m— Anne

PILLAGE

OBERT SKYE

SHADOW
MOUNTAIN

To those who still watch the skies

Library of Congress Cataloging-in-Publication Data

Skye, Obert.
    Pillage / Obert Skye.
    p. cm.
    Summary: Upon his mother's death, fifteen-year-old Beck Phillips is sent to live with an eccentric uncle he had never met in a remote manor house, where he learns that his family suffers from a curse that allows him to make plants grow on command and dragon eggs hatch.
    ISBN 978-1-59038-922-5 (hardcover : alk. paper)
  [1. Magic—Fiction. 2. Blessing and cursing—Fiction. 3. Eccentrics and eccentricities—Fiction. 4. Dragons—Fiction. 5. Uncles—Fiction. 6. Household employees—Fiction. 7. Identity—Fiction.] I. Title.
    PZ7.S62877Pil 2008
    [Fic]—dc22

                                       2008005419

Printed in the United States of America
Worzalla Publishing Co., Stevens Point, WI

10   9   8   7   6   5   4   3   2   1

CONTENTS

"Then what about dragons?" I questioned, finally getting to the question I really wanted to ask.

Aeron stopped looking out the window and gazed at me. His hands shook slightly and I could see a dark change in his eyes. It was as obvious as black clouds gathering for a deadly storm.

"Dragons?" he whispered dryly.

"Dragons," I said firmly.

Aeron breathed out slowly, letting his shoulders drop. "Dragons," he finally said. "Well, unfortunately, they are a far different thing."

CHAPTER 1

Kind and Clever Hooligan

I SHOULDN'T HAVE SAID IT, but the word slipped out of my mouth as easy as air. It wasn't exactly the kind of word any well-behaved student would use, which sort of explained why I had just used it. And it certainly isn't the most elegant way to start off a story, but it honestly represents what I was feeling. Besides, I could have said something a lot stronger. But not everybody wants to read a story with those kinds of words and thoughts being expressed in the very first sentence.

"Stop swearing," Jason screamed.

"Then stop pushing," I yelled back. "I'm pinned in."

Jason pushed again.

"Seriously," I snapped. "I'm stuck."

"Then let's crawl out!" he yelled back. "It's too dark to see anymore."

"I can't move," I insisted. "I'm really stuck."

The "I" and the "I'm" in both those sentences was me: Beck Phillips. I hate to talk about myself, but a few bits of information might be helpful. I'm fifteen, but I'll be sixteen in three months. Which makes me fifteen and three-quarters, but only a child would describe it that way—and I don't think of myself as a child. Unless of course you are using the word *child* as in, "He's an only child."

In that case, it's completely true.

I am an only child with an unbalanced single mother. I suppose both of those things could have something to do with the mess I was in, but my mother, Francine, watches a lot of *Oprah* so I've heard how "it's important for people to take responsibility for their own actions."

That said, I, Beck Phillips, take full responsibility for being stuck in my school's pitch-black venting system with my friend, Jason, behind me and a garbage bag full of angry bees in front of me.

The idea had seemed so simple: bag the huge beehive that had been hanging low in a fast-growing tree near my apartment, release it into the school's ventilation system, and enjoy a couple of days off as they try to exterminate the pests. Jason thought we should release the assailants at the vent's outside opening, but I believe "a job worth doing is worth doing well." Again, my mom watches a lot of *Oprah*.

So I insisted we crawl into the ducts as far as possible. That way we could achieve maximum pandemonium. My insistence now seemed stupid. In fact, the entire plan was beginning to feel foolish.

I'd like to say I was simply doing what I was doing to make everyone's life more exciting, but even I didn't believe that. In the words of my school's counselor, I was acting out to be heard. She thought that because I had moved around so much and attended so many different schools no one ever really got to know me. She thought that my subconscious didn't enjoy this. She thought that's why I was "acting out." I thought she, like my mother, watched too much *Oprah*.

Of course, there may have been some truth to what she said. After all, I had been at this school for a month and I don't think anyone aside from Jason knew my name. I didn't have a grudge against any single student, I was just tired of being invisible. I figured this would get my name out there.

Beck Phillips, bee wrangler.

Had I been standing out in the open on a sunny day I would look like most almost-sixteen-year-old boys. My brown hair is a bit too long and hangs over my ears; it blocks about twenty percent of what my brown eyes take in. My ears stick out a bit and

I probably have more confidence than a person in my shoes should. I'm taller than most guys my age and even though I'm never one to brag I should point out that a seventeen-year-old girl at the community pool told her friend that I was cute.

"I'm not staying in here, Beck," Jason panicked, bringing me back to the situation at hand. "I'm getting out."

"Quiet," I said firmly. "Someone will hear us. We're probably right above Mr. Shin's class."

"I don't care," Jason said. "This stinks. I never wanted to do this anyway."

"But you are," I pointed out, still trying to free myself from the tight duct. "Now pull me out, I can't move!"

"No," Jason said.

"I'm stuck," I hissed. "Pull me out."

"No."

I could hear Jason begin to move away, backing down the duct.

"You can't just leave me," I said as quietly as my worried soul would let me. "Some friend."

"Whatever," Jason said. "I barely know you, Beck."

Jason was right about that. He was a skinny kid with big teeth and a large, flat forehead. He seemed to wear a lot of green shirts and his father worked for the city auditing books. I had met Jason while playing basketball at the park. I was desperately trying to impress a couple of girls with my moves when I ran into him crossing the court. We fell to the ground, got up and yelled at each other for a couple of minutes, and then decided it would probably be easier to be friends. We weren't terribly alike, but I thought that, with enough time, we could get along.

Apparently, I was wrong.

"I'll tell them it was your idea," I yelled, not able to keep my voice down any longer. "You'll be busted for sure."

If Jason replied I couldn't hear it. He was long gone. He had left me alone, in a dark duct with a bag full of increasingly ticked-off bees.

"Nice," I mumbled to myself. "Thanks a lot, jerk."

I thought about yelling for help, but I still wasn't convinced that I couldn't find a way out of the situation unscathed. My right hand was stretched out in front of me holding the cinched black bag and my left arm was pinned to my left side. I twisted my legs, trying to get some movement, but I was stuck tight. Sweat began to slowly and annoyingly drip down into my eyes.

"Perfect."

I breathed deep, trying not to panic.

"I'm going to die here," I said nervously, halfway believing it. "What a nice way—"

Thwump!

Somewhere behind me the heat kicked on. Almost instantly

large waves of warm air washed through and around my captive body. The sweat dripping into my eyes increased but I couldn't reach to wipe it away.

"I'm in trouble," I said needlessly into the warm dark.

I remembered some teacher at one of the many schools I had been shuffled through over my life having said something about heat making things expand. With that tiny bit of vague knowledge, I begged the universe to please expand the metal duct currently trapping me. In return, I promised not to release the bees.

The duct didn't expand.

I upped my commitment and promised I would start to care about others and I would try not to swear so much.

The duct felt even tighter. I could feel myself cooking.

"Son of a . . ." I stopped myself.

I made one last promise, but even before I finished it in my head, I knew I wouldn't keep that particular promise.

I closed my eyes, hoping that in my last moments of life some wise wizard would appear to me in my delirium and invite me to enter a portal to some place much cooler and filled with light.

The sweat on my face and skin felt like boiling water. My head rang from the noise of the hot air. I began to thrash and scream. I would have liked to go out in a much braver and dignified way, but I couldn't take it anymore. I hollered as loud as I could, hoping someone would hear and come to my rescue. In my state of panic and confusion I mistakenly forgot how important it was to keep holding onto the bag. I began to beat my fists against the side of the duct.

"Somebody! Help!"

The furnace stopped. I couldn't see anything in the dark, but the cooler air felt like a positive sign.

"Hello!" I yelled. "Anyone!"

I thought I could hear someone hollering far away down another duct. I stopped yelling to listen.

I remembered the bees.

Something light tickled my right arm at the same moment tiny wings brushed against my nose. I grabbed for the bag in the dark, but the heat moving through the vent had blown it just out of my reach. My heart began to beat so hard I could hear it pounding against the metal duct.

I don't like bees. I never have. I find their tiny striped bodies to be as frightening as almost anything I had ever seen in a horror movie. Now, thanks to my panic, the bag was open and the bees were free. I could feel more and more of them moving up my arm. I knew if I moved it would only make things worse, so I kept still, forced to endure the horrid feeling of prickly bee feet inching their way up my arm.

They made it to my face.

One crawled over my lips and down my neck.

"Heeeellp," I tried to scream through the corner of my sealed lips. "Heeeeeelpp meeee."

My plea came out like a slow leak.

Bees began moving under my collar and down the back of my neck. I could hear them buzzing near my ears. Their wings sounded like a hundred chain saws. I had been mad at myself for wishing the heat would turn off. Now I wanted it to flip back on and blow the bees away.

I could feel one on my ankle.

It was too much. The sweat on my face and the thousands of tiny legs crawling over me was more than I could take. I'd always thought if I were ever faced with some terrible situation I would take the high road and bravely make the best of it.

It turns out that's not true.

I went from a boy of fifteen and three-quarters to a child of five and a half in an instant. I screamed like a tiny kid getting his hair pulled by the monster under the bed. I violently kicked my legs and bucked my body up and down as hard as I could.

Apparently the bees didn't like that. I could feel them sting my ankle, my cheek, my arm, and my back.

I freaked out.

I rocked so hard I knocked my right shoulder out of joint and banged my head against the duct. All I could hear was the noise of me shouting and what sounded like two billion bees shouting back at me.

I suppose it was lucky for me that most heating ducts weren't designed to hold the weight of a person. I felt fortunate—I also felt the duct break loose beneath my waist. My right leg slipped out. I kicked harder, banging my head with such force that I could see stars and hear the sound of angels screaming.

The duct floor beneath my head broke open and the weight of my body shifted wildly as the entire section came loose. I could feel a terrible scraping on my right hip as the bottom dropped out from under me. The section of broken duct crashed down against a large counter filled with dishes and bottles. I would have fallen with the duct had it not been for the large metal seam where the duct had once been attached catching at the waistband of my jeans. I dangled from the vent like a human piñata.

Bees burst out of the broken vent and into the room. I could see I had been wrong about a couple of things: one, I was not above Mr. Shin's room. I was above Miss Harpthorn's home economics class. And two, it had not been a bunch of angels screaming, but a large group of girls—some of the very girls I had once unimpressed on a basketball court.

Miss Harpthorn and her class looked up at me like I was a

mangled animal that had come to life to attack them. I was about to say something so funny that it would have put everyone at ease and made the whole situation nothing but a great story, but just then my pants ripped, sending me pants-less down onto a counter full of dishes and surrounded by far too many eyewitnesses.

Bees swarmed through the room. I closed my eyes and prayed I was dreaming. I opened them just in time to witness a fat bee sting the tip of my nose. I screamed and swatted at the bee as I fell off the counter onto the hard linoleum floor. A broken dish sliced a long cut along my right arm.

The room was filled with girls screaming and bees buzzing. I felt a strange sense of accomplishment. Someone grabbed me by my cut arm and tried to pull me up. I shifted and turned, sitting up on my rear. Whoever was helping me let go. I looked up and saw the large face of Principal Spools.

"Beck, are you okay?" he asked, his red face simmering.

A fistful of bees flew between us.

"I think so."

"I've been looking for you," he said sadly, sounding way too calm after what I had just done.

"I was in the duct."

He reached his hand out and I took it. He pulled me to my feet.

"You were looking for me?" I questioned, wondering if Jason had crawled out and told on me immediately.

"Something's happened," he said loudly, swatting at bees with his hand.

I wanted to say, "Duh," but his tone of voice indicated he was referring to something *besides* me releasing bees into the school and falling pants-less into the girls' cooking class.

"Come with me," he said much more compassionately than I expected.

"What is it?" I asked nervously.

Principal Spools said nothing, moving me out of the room and into the hall. The school was alive with students running for the exits and batting at bees in the air. Girls and boys alike were screaming and frantically looking for any way out.

I was torn. Part of me felt as if I had accomplished something big. I had created a mess. My body ached from the fall as well as from the cuts and bee stings, but I could walk. I should have been proud. But the truth was Operation a Couple of Days Off had failed miserably. And unbeknownst to me there was still a large dose of pain in my immediate future.

It's interesting how something as bad as what I had done could be overlooked and almost forgotten because of the death of someone I loved.

Hermitage Pillage was born in Scotland in the year 1751. He was a kind and honest man who possessed a remarkable ability to grow things. He farmed his entire life, wanting nothing more than to work the land and assure his family's happiness. Hermitage died peacefully in his modest home. His wife, Hope, whom he loved dearly, passed away in her sleep three days later. They were survived by two daughters and one son. Their son's name was Edward.

Excerpt from section one of The Grim Knot, *as recorded by Daniel Phillips*

CHAPTER 2

I'm Miserable Now

I WATCHED THE FAT DROPS OF RAIN roll down the car windows like frightened tears, darting side to side and mixing quickly with the tracks of drops that had streamed down moments before. The beating of the rain on the car's roof was thunderous. I wondered if my life would ever be silent again.

My eyes burned and my head ached from trying not to cry. I could see through the wet window that my mother's coffin was being lowered slowly into the ground by the aid of two thick yellow straps. There was a small blue tent over the grave, protecting the coffin and the tiny group of shivering people looking on.

"Pointless," I whispered. I didn't care how much protection or cover was available. Even if a single drop of rain never touched my skin, I knew my soul was going to be wet for some time.

My mother had not been well. My father had left us when I was an infant and my mom couldn't hold down a job. She couldn't remember to pay bills or buy groceries. We were constantly getting kicked out of apartments because she couldn't remember to turn off the bathtub water or the gas on the stove. I tried to help, but each year as she grew more confused it became harder for her to even have me around. She knew I was there, but I'm pretty sure it only made her feel trapped.

There had been state workers and cops who had worried about my welfare, but in the end they had other cases to concern themselves with and I was always able to stay out of their control.

The last few months had been the worst for my mother. She had gone to the doctor just last week to get some new pills. It was now painfully obvious those pills had not worked.

I watched the casket disappear below the horizon. Once it was out of sight, a short dark man in overalls and carrying a shovel appeared out of nowhere. I watched as he dug the shovel into a nearby pile of dirt. The shovel sliced into the soil and then the man tossed the large lumps of earth down into the hole. The mourners slowly drifted off to mourn someplace less wet.

"It was a lovely service," Mr. Claude said soothingly, placing his left hand on my shoulder. "Very nice indeed."

I looked over at the man sitting next to me in the backseat of the car. Mr. Claude was a thin man with ruddy skin and unnaturally black hair. He wore a gold tie and a black suit that was as faded as the life that had just been honored. Mr. Claude was my mother's lawyer. I had never understood why she needed a lawyer in the first place, but she said it was because of her family. I had only met him twice before and now I was forced to share one of the worst moments of my life with him.

"There was nothing lovely about it," I argued.

"Well, the flowers were beautiful," he sniffed.

"Flowers?" I said incredulously. "Who are you?"

Mr. Claude's face reddened a bit and he straightened his already straight tie. The rain became even heavier, making it impossible for there to be a truly awkward silence. Eventually Mr. Claude spoke again.

"Beck, this may not be the best time, but I suppose there is no best time for what must be said."

I stared at Mr. Claude and wished he would disappear. It didn't work.

"Your mother was financially strapped at the time of her death," he said as though it were some great surprise.

You mean us moving to a poor neighborhood and me having to go to

a crummy school and get free lunch wasn't just her trying to be humble?
That's what I wanted to say. Instead I sarcastically said, "Really?"

Mr. Claude sniffed.

"Fortunately for you, she comes from money."

The words made no sense to me. I pictured a large pile of money giving birth to her.

"What?" I asked.

"Her family was wealthy."

"Rich?"

"I suppose."

"And they're sending money?" I asked hopefully.

I had been spending the last few days sleeping at my neighbor's house. Mrs. Welch was a kind old woman who had befriended us the second we moved in. When she heard my mother passed away, she instantly insisted I stay with her until they could figure out where I would be best placed.

Best placed.

I loved whenever I heard someone say that—like I was a puzzle piece or a vase that people simply needed to find a spot for.

"They are not sending money," Mr. Claude said. "But she has a brother. He's sent for you."

He said it so casually I thought he might be joking. So I laughed.

"You're kidding, right?"

"No," he insisted. "I'm quite serious. You are lucky to have someplace to go. If not for your uncle, you would be put into foster care until adopted. And I must say, Beck, the chance for adoption at your age is not stellar."

"I'm an orphan? What about my dad? He's got to be somewhere."

"We've made every attempt to find your father," Mr. Claude said with authority. "But there's no trace or clue as to where he is. It seems your mother has had no contact with him since he left. Nobody has."

"So I'm being sent away?"

"What did you expect?" he said dryly. "You've got no parents here."

It took everything I had in me to stop my eyes from dripping. I hadn't cried yet and I was in no mood to do so now. I let the anger I felt hold back the tears. I was tempted to get out of the car and just run away.

"Wait," I remembered. "You said my mom's brother is rich?"

"Your Uncle Aeron is very well off," Mr. Claude said. "I've seen pictures of his estate and it is quite astounding."

"Did you bring the pictures?" I asked greedily.

"No, no," Mr. Claude waved. "It didn't seem appropriate."

"Of course not," I muttered. "Why show me where I'm going?"

"Listen, Beck, you'd do well to work on your manners," Mr. Claude said boldly. "I'm certain your uncle will not tolerate such sharpness."

"I'll try to be dull," I said. "So where am I going?"

"Kingsplot is a couple of days travel from here, but there's a single-rail line that goes all the way" he said. "Your uncle has graciously sent a train ticket for you."

"How nice of him," I said bitterly. "I can't just get on a train and go live with someone I've never met."

"It's either that or be put into a home here with someone you're not related to," he pointed out.

The rain on the roof simmered. It went from boisterous to beckoning, sounding like a soft whisper from Mother Nature herself. Most of the dirt that had been sitting next to my mother's grave was gone. I hated how I felt. I hated the dark inside of me that wanted nothing more than to break a window with my fist, or light something on fire, or . . .

Mr. Claude tapped on the glass dividing us from the driver. "To the train station," he ordered.

"Train station?" I asked with panic.

"I told you they've sent tickets."

"Today? I'm leaving today?"

"Well, you've got no place to stay," he pointed out. "Even your neighbor has run out of compassion for you. I guess she didn't enjoy you putting her wig on that stray dog."

"It was a joke," I defended.

"It was the final straw."

"I can't just leave," I argued, feeling like I needed to be where my mother was buried. She was all I had. "Don't make me leave her."

"You'll feel better once you're traveling," Mr. Claude said. "I promise."

"What about my stuff?" I asked, wondering how he could promise me how I'd feel.

"The few things you had are packed and waiting at the station," he said. "As your mother wished."

"She knew she was going to die now?"

"She knew it was inevitable." He sniffed again. "She also knew it would be best to make it as easy for you as possible."

"What about my plant?"

"What plant?" Mr. Claude scoffed.

The plant in question was a large-leafed fern I had raised from a tiny seedling. It had meant a ton to me during the last month. It was the one living thing that responded to me and was better off because I was around.

"*My* plant," I argued. "Mrs. Welch has it."

"I'm sure she'll take good care of it," Mr. Claude said callously. "Move on, driver."

"But—"

"It's a plant," Mr. Claude said soothingly. "The world is full of plants."

I felt angry. The world wasn't full of my plants. My world at the moment wasn't full of anything but pain. I had loved my mother and now the only person who had ever had any patience or love for me was gone and I was being forced to move away.

The driver put the car into gear and pulled slowly away from the graveside.

I don't care what you say; I had every right to cry.

Edward Pillage was not at all like his father. He cared only for himself and for money. Edward used the Pillage gift of growing to amass great wealth and power. In a few short years, he had become one of the richest men in Scotland.

Excerpt from section two of The Grim Knot, *as recorded by Daniel Phillips*

CHAPTER 3

Nowhere Fast

I THREW MY BACKPACK ONTO the red cloth seat and plopped down next to it. The backpack and an old suitcase in the storage cart made up my entire entourage. I owned surprisingly little in my life besides the black shirt and jeans I was currently wearing.

An old man and a young girl sat across from me in the train compartment. From the way they sat, it was obvious that they didn't know one another. The old man was nose deep into a magazine. He had a half-bald head and a full beard. The girl was at least my age and looked both bored and bothered that I was what she would be staring at for the next little while.

"It could be worse," I tried, smiling a half smile at her.

The girl looked at me as if she were unsure of what language I was speaking.

"I mean I could be some deranged fat guy who smelled."

It took a moment, but like waiting for a stubborn sunrise, her smile eventually appeared across the bottom of her face. She was the prettiest girl I had seen in a long time.

"I'm Beck," I said.

"Kate," she replied coolly.

"Hi, Kate."

She sort of waved.

"How far are you going?" I asked.

"The end of the line," she answered.

"Kingsplot?"

Kate nodded.

"Me too," I said much too excitedly to come off sounding cool.

Her sunrise smile faded but that didn't stop me from staring. She was beautiful in a farmer's daughter, spelling-bee champion kind of way. She had long red hair that was partially held back by a thin black headband. Her skin was as white as my knuckles had been the second before I fell from the vent. She wore a plaid skirt and long white knee-high socks. Her white shirt was mostly covered by a thick black sweater. She looked caught between styles, as if she had been preppy but was slowly switching to hippie. Her eyes watched the scenery outside.

"It's far," she added. "Very far."

"I'm going to live there," I said cleverly.

"That's great," she replied, not bothering to turn and look at me.

I missed her smile.

"I have no idea what it's like there," I said, hoping she did.

"I'm sure you'll get to know it."

"So, that's your home?"

"Yes," she said flatly.

The train jerked forward, grunting and hissing. I didn't like the movement. I felt like I was abandoning my mom and the little bit of life I had lived here.

The half-bald man in our compartment set his magazine down and rubbed the point where his nose met his eyebrows. He looked tired and concerned about having to travel in the company of two teenagers.

I watched the landscape speed up outside. In a few minutes the world was washing by in a stream of color and stretching images. I thought about the last time I had seen my mother alive. It had been the morning of the bee incident. I had complained to her that I needed some money and she had slurred something about how everyone wants more than they have. I tried to move the words around in my head to make it seem as if she had said something less profound and more personal.

"So, it's a nice place?" I asked Kate. "Kingsplot?"

Kate looked at me and then over to the old guy. She appeared confused by the fact that I was still talking to her. I suddenly wished I was a fat deranged man that smelled just to get back at her.

"All right," I said strongly. "I guess I'll just talk to myself from now on."

Kate yawned and the old man pulled his coat up over his head and pushed his body back into the seat.

"This is my first train ride," I said, mostly to myself.

"My father doesn't trust planes," she said shortly. "He has no problem sending his daughter to visit a bunch of unknown relatives in a big city, but he's concerned about me flying home."

I stared at her for a moment and then said, "My father left when I was about one."

Kate shrugged and yawned again.

A man in a blue uniform wearing a cap two sizes too big for his head stepped into our compartment.

"Are we all in the right spots?" he asked as if we were babies in numbered cribs.

I showed him my ticket and he looked at the others.

"Don't open the window," he insisted. "The windows along this entire section have not worked properly ever since the train derailed a month ago. The entire frame has twisted just a bit."

I couldn't think of a single reason why he should be telling us that.

"So windows closed," he continued. "And if you need assistance there will be an attendant one car down."

"Are there any vacancies on the train?" the older man asked.

"I believe we have one empty seat two cars up."

The man gathered his stuff as quickly as he could and scurried from the compartment as fast as a rat abandoning a sinking ship.

"Have a pleasant trip," the uniformed man said to us.

"I can't see how we couldn't," I answered sarcastically.

The attendant's smile looked forced. Kate simply yawned again.

I had never been on a train before and the clack of the wheels as they sped forward was oddly intoxicating. Each mile we traveled my eyelids became increasingly heavy. I tried to fight it, but sleep was smothering me. I said a couple of clever things to Kate and she replied in unkind.

I shifted my backpack and stretched out on the empty seat next to me. I pushed my head up against the small pillow the train company had provided. There was a musty smell in the cabin that made it seem even more uncomfortable than it was. I breathed slowly and could smell a trace of smoke. I would have opened my eyes to investigate it, but my mind was sick of being awake. I had not slept well ever since my mom had died. My body felt like it was in the mood to make up for lost time. I fell asleep instantly.

When I woke up, Kate was staring at me. Despite my open eyes my body still felt like it was asleep.

"Did I snore?" I asked sleepily.

"And drooled," she said disgusted.

I wiped at my mouth and moved to sit up. My head weighed a hundred pounds. I shifted and my head fell back down against the seat. I tried to blink the sleep and pain out through my eye sockets.

"I don't feel so great," I said.

"Maybe that's why you slept so long," Kate suggested.

"How long?"

"Twelve hours."

"What?" I said in shock, sitting up. My head wobbled like a large melon with an off-balance center. "Whoa."

"You slept for about twelve hours," Kate said again. "You slept through five stops, dinner, and unless you get up and move it you'll miss breakfast. They stop serving it at nine-thirty."

"I can't believe it."

My stomach growled out loud.

"Maybe your stomach will convince you."

"Where are we now?" I asked, looking out the window.

"About two hours from Kingsplot."

The scenery was green all over. Tall trees grew along the tracks and stretched their branches over the train creating a tunnel of foliage and making the cabin dark for the time of day. Through the breaks in the trees I could see a dull blue lake and mountains taller than the window would allow me to take in. I might have found the view interesting, but my mind was quick to remind me that being on the train at all was the result of my loss.

I felt depressed and sick.

Kate closed her eyes and leaned back. I hoped she would fall asleep and begin to drool. I lifted my backpack up off the floor and onto the empty seat next to me. I unzipped the main compartment and pulled out a thin book. It was a worn journal that my mother had written in sporadically over the last few years of her life. I had read most of it while waiting for the train but none of it made sense and holding it depressed me even more.

There was a small picture pretending to be a bookmark on page twenty-seven. It was a picture of my mother when she was young and happy. In the picture she was pretty and looked like a walking beam of light. There was a man with her. I assumed he was my father. He looked smart, and in love with my mom. I hated him for leaving us.

I pulled out another picture of my mother from my backpack. It had been taken a month before she died. She looked like a different person than the young girl in the other photo. Her dirty blonde hair was tied back with a green felt tie and rogue strands of hair were twisting and wriggling in all directions. Her cheeks were permanently red and she was straining to smile. She was wearing a blue robe over a white T-shirt and sweatpants. Her feet were bare and her toenails were speckled with chipped red nail polish.

I missed her.

In the history of mothers there had certainly been better, but in fairness to history there had most certainly been worse.

The train began to pull and jerk upward.

"We're going up?" I asked.

Kate kept her eyes closed and any response to herself. I stood up as the train continued to pull forward and upward. I steadied myself by holding onto the plastic strap hanging from the wall. I could see the trees through the window beginning to slant at a slight angle as the train slowly climbed a mountain path.

"I'm going out," I announced. "Do you want anything?"

I took her silence as a no.

The train's hallway was empty. The red paisley carpet looked busy and out of fashion. I walked down the corridor looking for a bathroom. The cabin next to mine was vacant as were the next two. I used the bathroom at the end of the car and then pushed through the doors leading to the dining car. The tables were empty. A wrinkled and scrawny man stood behind a bar wiping the counter down.

"Am I too late for breakfast?"

He nodded toward a basket of muffins at the end of the bar.

"Anything else?"

He repeated his nod.

I grabbed a muffin and took a big bite. I could taste cold, bitter blueberries.

"Umm," I said. "Where is everyone?"

He kept wiping down the counter, acting as if I hadn't asked him anything. I decided since he wouldn't answer me that I would go looking for myself. I moved through the dining car and into a section of sleeper compartments. The train lurched forward with hard, jarring motions.

The doors to all of the sleeper compartments were open but the compartments were empty. My insides began to feel more than just hunger. Something wasn't right. I had fallen asleep and woken up on an empty train. The next car was filled with nothing but empty seats. The same attendant who had checked my ticket earlier entered the car from the other direction. He was surprised to see me.

"Yes?" he asked.

"I'm just walking around," I said, looking past him.

"It's best that the passengers stay in their designated seats."

"What passengers?" I asked.

"Not many people travel to Kingsplot."

"Can't I walk around?" I asked.

"I think not."

"Can I see the captain?" I said, trying to sound young and interested in how trains run.

"That would be the *engineer*," the attendant corrected. "And no. It is best for the safety of everyone if you return to your seat."

I'm old enough to know how futile it is to argue with some adults. I turned and walked back through the car and into the dining car.

The attendant followed me.

"I can find my way," I said.

Apparently there is no course in train etiquette that teaches its students to be cordial. The attendant simply shooed me forward. I reached my compartment and stepped inside. I closed the sliding door behind me. Kate looked up at me and blinked.

"There's nobody else on the train," I whispered.

"What?"

"The train's empty."

"Who's driving it?"

"Someone, but all the passengers are gone."

"Well, not many people ride this train to the end."

I didn't like the way she said, "the end."

"And we're moving upward."

"Into the mountains," she agreed. "Kingsplot is in the Hagen Valley."

"You're not bothered that there are no other people on board?"

Kate shrugged.

"I went through three cars—there was nobody but a waiter."

"Maybe they're all in the cars behind us."

"Maybe."

I slid the door back open. I stepped into the hall and looked up and down it. The attendant was gone.

"He's not there."

"Who?"

"The ticket dude."

"I thought you said everyone was gone."

The train seemed to be moving faster.

"The ticket dude's still here," I said. "Who else is going to check the tickets of all the missing passengers? I'm going to check the compartments behind me. Wanna come?"

Her look told me she didn't, but her knees appeared to be

lifting her up. She stood next to me at the door. I was so surprised she had taken me up on my offer that I froze.

"Well?" she said.

It was interesting to see her standing. Kate was two inches shorter than me and her hair looked longer than I'd first suspected. From this angle she didn't look quite so bored to be alive. I slipped into the hall and began to creep down the hallway. I kept my hands against the walls to balance myself as I walked. I looked back every couple of seconds to make sure Kate hadn't left me.

"I'm still here," she said, after my fourth glance.

All the compartments were empty. The next car was the same way. So was the one after that.

"Don't you think this is weird?"

Kate shrugged. Her action, or lack thereof, reminded me of my mother. For as long as I could remember, my mother had responded to me more with shrugs and grunts than with any real conversation. I felt right at home.

The next car was also empty.

"See?" I said anxiously.

"No one else is going to Kingsplot," Kate said casually. "Big deal."

The trees outside the train became thicker and darkened the inside of the train even more.

"I think it's weird," I said.

"I think you watch too much TV," Kate said. "I'm going back."

"Two more cars," I said. "There has to be someone."

Kate sighed in resignation.

The next two cars were empty and the last one was locked with a sign above the door that read Baggage. The car we were now in had a partially glass ceiling, giving us a terrific view of the tree branches reaching and weaving over the train. It also made me feel that each mile forward was closing up the space we had just traveled. I felt like we were being zipped up into the mountains.

"No passengers. Only one attendant."

"You're forgetting that we're passengers," Kate pointed out.

"You don't think this feels wrong?"

"It feels like we're on a train climbing up a mountain. I'm going back to my seat."

"Why?" I asked. "You can sit anywhere."

"My ticket says 32A."

Who could argue with that?

Kate walked out of the car and back toward our compartment. I stayed to look up through the glass ceiling. The foliage was growing thicker every clack of the track. I sat down in one of the many empty seats and tried not to think about my mom.

She had not always been so out of it. I could remember a time many years ago when I had mattered to her. Unfortunately those memories were harder to pull up than the ones where she was ill and neglectful.

I stood up and began to work my way back. As I stepped into the next car I was surprised to see a single passenger sitting in one of the seats. She was an old woman with a feathery hat and a purple purse that she clutched tightly in her lap. She looked at me as though I was going to steal not only her purse, but her hat as well.

I walked past her, nodding a cautious hello, and entered the next car. The rest of the train was vacant until I made it to our compartment and noticed that in the compartment next to ours there was a man sitting alone with his head down and his arms crossed against his chest. I watched him for a moment and realized he was sleeping.

I stepped past his compartment and slipped into ours. Kate was sitting, looking out the window. She turned and looked at me as I entered.

Our relationship was growing.

"There are a couple of other passengers now," I whispered fiercely. "Two of them."

"Wow."

"Seriously," I said. "Where'd they come from? We haven't stopped."

"I don't know, Nancy Drew," Kate said, looking out the window again. "The bathroom?"

"Whatever," I said, embarrassed. "I still think it's weird."

The train choked as it moved up the mountain pass. The windows began to blur with small drops of water. The water swirled around the window in wispy gray patterns.

"It's raining?" I asked, stepping to the window and looking up. The trees were so thick above and around us that it felt like a tunnel of branches and leaves. I couldn't understand how any rain could even reach us.

"It's the mist," Kate said. "Kingsplot and these mountains are always covered with mist and fog."

I looked back out the window.

"It's because of the lakes," Kate added.

"I need sunshine," I said, having lived most of my life in the West.

"You'll be pale and vitamin D-deficient in no time."

"Great."

Kate sighed and grimaced.

I'm not sure why that made me happy. I suppose it could have something to do with the way her blue eyes looked when she grimaced at me.

"Where do you live?" I asked.

Kate opened her mouth to speak just as the train began to pick up speed. "We're getting close," she said instead of answering my question. "We're entering the valley."

"And you live in the valley?" I tried again.

"I live way up in the mountains," she said snottily.

Kate gathered her few things and put them into her bag. The windows lit up as the trees thinned a bit. I could see fields and lakes through the forest. A weathered white barn with roses covering one entire wall sat in a field of thick green growth.

Kate stood up and waved a small wave from her hip. I think it was directed toward me.

"See you," she said, and with that she was out the door and walking down the corridor.

"Wait!"

She didn't.

"Nice meeting you, too," I said to myself.

The train was still moving at the same fast pace and there was no sign of us pulling into any town or dwelling. I sat in my seat and tried to figure out how to feel. I was excited to be doing something new, but I was nervous to be doing it without my mother. Even though she had been sick or confused all the time, taking care of her had always helped me move into new situations. I think the routine of me watching out for her helped keep my mind busy.

Now that routine was gone. Amplifying my feelings of uneasiness was the feeling the train gave me. It didn't seem right. I felt like I was riding through an old Hollywood set that had been built to use in a movie. And the missing passengers only added to my uneasiness and heightened my desire to rethink what I was doing. Of course I didn't have many options. I could have gone into foster care or taken the crazy train.

The train began to slow down as we approached the station in Kingsplot. I could see cobblestone streets and quaint buildings with shingled roofs. The trees were still all around, but they were different and taller. They had thin white trunks and bushy foliage. I could see a large fountain shaped like a roaring lion at the far end of a wide road. Behind the fountain rose a tall pillar with a large clock on it.

The streets looked busy. Pockets of red flowers filled window boxes and flowerpots placed randomly around town.

The train started to shiver slowly and, like a dying snake, it slithered into the station and gave up the ghost. I stood up and grabbed my backpack.

"Last stop," the attendant hollered as he came down the corridor. "Kingsplot, last stop."

I stepped out of the compartment and looked at him.

"They pay you for this?" I asked.

"Last stop. Kingsplot. Last stop," he hollered into my face as he walked off.

I walked down the corridor and off the train. I couldn't see Kate anywhere. She had gotten off fast. There was an old man handing out suitcases. I took mine.

It was only then that I realized I had no idea who I was looking for, or what to do next.

In the year of 1809, Edward Pillage married a woman by the name of Lucinda and they eventually had three children—two girls and a boy. Their son was named Bruno. Sadly, Edward had no affection for his daughters, but he cared deeply for his son. Aside from accruing wealth and power, Bruno was the only thing Edward had an interest in.

Excerpt from section two of The Grim Knot, *as recorded by Daniel Phillips*

CHAPTER 4

Up to the Old House

THE TRAIN PULLED AWAY, MOVING backward and leaving me standing alone on the platform. The two other passengers had disappeared, having places to go and things to do. The clock on the train station pointed out clearly that it was twelve-thirteen. Although it was just past high noon, the mist in the gray air made it seem much later.

I stood with my suitcase and backpack wondering what in the world I was doing. It was cold and I wished I had brought a jacket or a long-sleeved shirt. I actually missed the heating duct I had gotten caught in. At least it had been warm there and I had known where I was.

I looked out the large archway into the city streets. Through the mist I could see people walking up and down the cobble-stone walkways, doing business or talking to others. Kingsplot was alive and busy. The only lull in activity was the train plat-form where I stood.

A thick flume of mist pushed through the air, blocking my view of the archway and making me feel like a pointed island in the middle of a foggy ocean.

I stepped forward just as the sound of knocking echoed around me. I looked around; nothing but fog.

Again with the knocking.

The fog was getting thicker. I couldn't tell if the noise was coming from behind me or in front of me so I moved to the side of the archway as if to step out of the way of whatever was mak-ing the noise.

The knocking grew louder. Thump. Pause. Thump.

I could see the tall form of someone or something material-izing in the fog. I moved back, clutching my backpack and hop-ing whoever was coming was both kind and filled with information that would help me know what to do.

The form stepped out of the fog and stopped directly in front of me. The shape belonged to a tall man with thin shoul-ders and crooked legs. He wore a felt cap and a vest that was buttoned up. His shirtsleeves were long and white. He looked at me with dark black eyes and a smile so buried that it would take pliers to pull it out. He had a bulbous nose and ears that stuck out just like mine. In his right hand was the cane that had been the cause of all the commotion.

"Mr. Phillips?" he asked, his voice as flat as glass.

"I think so," I said, confused.

"Are you or are you not Francine's boy?"

Hearing my mother's name made me feel worse. "Yes," I answered.

He looked at my single suitcase. "Is there more?" he asked.

I shook my head and he extended his hand to take the handle of my suitcase.

"Welcome," he said. "My name is Thomas. This way please."

I stayed directly behind Thomas, afraid of losing him in the mist. He walked slowly, moving through the archway and down around the station. We stepped into an open courtyard bursting with rosebushes. The bushes looked weighed down by the gray and wet weather.

Outside of the courtyard there was a large black car. It surprised me to see it. The town of Kingsplot had such an old feeling that to see something modern looked out of place.

Thomas opened the back door and I climbed in. He loaded the luggage into the trunk and then got behind the wheel, sliding his cane into the passenger seat. He turned to look back at me.

"Have I welcomed you?" he asked.

"Yes," I answered.

"Of course," he sighed heavily. "Sit back. The ride will take about an hour."

"An hour?" I said, surprised by the length of time.

"The manor sits well above the town."

Manor? I liked the sound of that.

"So, is it always this wet?"

"Always," he answered, pulling the black car out onto the main street and driving slowly through the town.

The street was lined with ivy-covered buildings and small shops that sold individual items. One sold shoes, one sold hats, and another sold vacuums. I looked around for a McDonald's or a Wal-Mart, but there was nothing of the sort within view. I couldn't even see a gas station or a freeway.

"Do you have a Taco Bell here?" I asked.

"Certainly not," Thomas said, his voice tinged with insult.

"A mall?"

"There are strict covenants in Kingsplot," he replied as if that would clear it all up for me.

I had no idea what he meant, but I stopped asking questions.

We drove past a single tree standing behind a sign that read *Kingsplot, Quaint and Courteous.* I saw large homes that looked as old and regal as those in the movies. A girl was playing with a hula hoop, and I watched a milkman collect empty bottles from off a large back porch. The mist moved in weird patches and strips, making everything look slightly out of focus.

The homes became sparse and eventually disappeared altogether. Thomas followed the narrow road into the trees and up the side of the mountain. The car traveled the switchback road, rising in altitude. We passed through a long tunnel that was a touch too dark for my taste. Coming out of the tunnel we made a sharp turn that directed us even further up the mountain.

"How high are we going?"

Thomas didn't answer. Instead he slowed as another sharp corner slung us higher yet. We went through another tunnel that was not quite as long as the first and came out onto a flat shelf of green land. Two turns later I spotted a large house. It looked impressive enough to be called a manor. Massive granite lions guarded a winding driveway. My heart stopped, thinking this was where we were headed.

We passed it by without slowing.

I could see another building back in the woods. It had more chimneys than I could count and a vast front lawn. Two men carrying shotguns crossed the lawn with dead birds in their grip.

We passed that driveway as well.

The mist was different at this height. It felt like we were inside a large patch of wet sky; everything looked greener and danker than in town. I could see a few birds flying through the soggy air. I worried about them flying over the gentlemen who were carrying shotguns.

Thomas reached up and pushed something near the driver's window visor. He coughed once as if signaling our arrival. I looked up ahead, wondering where we were. I could barely see two large ivy-covered gates begin to separate. It looked like the forest was opening itself up to swallow us whole. Near the gate was a small, empty shack with a clay-tiled roof. Three gargoyles were perched on the top of the gates, the two on the ends reaching down with their claws and the one in the center reaching up. I looked out the back window of the car and my breath was stolen by how far we'd traveled. Through the low clouds and mist I could see Kingsplot miles below down in the valley.

"Wow."

The gates yawned and we drove through. The driveway was brick and lined with thick shrubs and odd statues. I could see a large house in the distance. It was back behind the trees with a pitched roof and three chimneys. It wasn't as enormous as the other mansions we had passed, but it was ten times larger than any place I thought I would ever live in.

"Is that it?" I asked, pointing through the front window.

"No," Thomas said. "Those are the stables."

The car followed the bend in the drive and the view parted

to reveal my uncle's mansion. I couldn't keep my jaw from falling open. The house was not a house, nor was it a mansion—it was somewhere between a mall and a castle. There were more chimneys and windows than any chimney or window store could ever possibly stock.

I counted at least seven floors.

The sixth floor of the manor was circled by a thick stone balcony, and the seventh floor sat back a bit with massive windows that were dark and shuttered.

The house was made of brown stone, and on each side of the mansion a tall bulb-shaped turret rose into the air like a tethered balloon. Wicked and mysterious-looking gargoyles circled each turret and lined the stone railing of the balcony. Centered on the very top of the mansion was a round, window-lined room capped by a large copper dome.

The car pulled around a spectacular fountain shaped like two huge serpents wrapped together. Water shot from their stone mouths in long strands, looking like wet forked tongues. We drove through a large breezeway to a back door that easily dwarfed every front door I had ever seen. It was obvious my uncle wasn't just wealthy; he was two steps beyond filthy, stinking rich.

I smiled, feeling happy for the first time in weeks.

Thomas stopped the car and got out. He shuffled around

the car and up the steps to the back door of the manor. I had expected him to help me get my luggage, but he only popped the trunk.

"Okay," I said to myself, stepping out of the car and onto the brick drive.

I looked up and marveled at the sheer height of the home. I felt like a toy action figure outside a playhouse. I half expected a huge hand to reach down and begin moving me around. I could see the gargoyles way up above, hanging out over the edge of the balcony, glaring down at me.

I got my luggage out of the trunk and stood there. Thomas appeared at the door and told me to hurry and come inside. I climbed the seven steps and entered. I shut the door behind me.

Inside, the walls were a dull blue. The ceiling was carved with what looked to be a map of the world. I was in a large hall-way that stretched at least fifty feet before turning a corner. To my right was a square doorway that opened into an enormous kitchen. I could see a fire burning in a spacious fireplace and a large wooden cutting block covered with dead birds. I wondered if they had been shot like the others I had seen.

Thomas clapped.

A woman with a lazy right eye and well-stained apron crawled out from a far corner of the kitchen and stared Thomas down with her one straight eye. She wasn't super fat, but she was completely padded, so much so that I felt she would have been perfectly unhurt if she were to be dropped from a six foot tall tower.

"Did you clap at me?" she asked Thomas with disdain.

"I wanted you to meet—"

"You clap at horses. Or after a decent show," she snipped. "This house has long since lost the opportunity to act snooty."

"The boy is—" Thomas tried to say.

"I can see that the boy's here," she simmered. "And thanks to you, he thinks it's perfectly acceptable to clap for my attention."

"Sorry, Millie," Thomas tried.

"Sorry?" Millie tisked, wiping her hands on her apron and turning her attention to me. "So. You're Francine's boy?"

"I am."

Millie looked me up and down like I was a piece of abstract art. She cocked her head and closed her bad eye.

"Smile for me," she asked.

"What?"

"Smile for me," she insisted.

I smiled as wide as I could.

"There it is!" she said happily, clapping her own hands. "It's been years since I've seen a Phillips' smile—blinding if done right."

"Thanks," I said, confused, but liking her all the same.

"Where are the others?" Thomas asked, trying to sound dignified again.

"How should I know?" Millie glared at him with both eyes. "Why don't you go clapping for them?"

Thomas stepped to a long rope that hung against the wall just inside the kitchen door. He pulled on it four times causing bells to ring throughout the house.

I thought about informing him that there were more sophisticated ways of communicating these days, but Thomas rang the bells with such authority that I didn't dare say anything.

In fact no one said anything. Thomas and Millie and I simply stood there in silence until I couldn't take it any longer.

"Is there a bathroom?"

"More than thirty of them," Millie said proudly.

"I only need one."

"Wait a moment," Thomas insisted. "Once you meet the staff you can go."

I couldn't wait to meet the staff.

Two minutes later a young woman with short hair and a shorter apron came walking quickly around the corner. The second she caught sight of me she smiled wide.

"Is this Beck?" she asked, walking right up to me and putting her arm around me.

"Of course," Millie said.

"Welcome," she smiled, looking at me like I was a horse she was thinking of buying. "I'm Wane."

"Really?" I asked without thinking.

"My father never really wanted children," she explained. "His feelings waned even more after my birth."

"Oh," I said, not understanding at all.

Wane smiled. "Look it up in the dictionary," she said kindly. "It'll make more sense then."

I had never used a dictionary in my entire life, but now I felt compelled to start.

"Wane will look after you," Thomas said.

"I will?" she questioned.

Thomas gave her a look that could have turned helium to stone.

"Of course I will," she agreed. "I've already contacted your school."

"School," I complained.

"It's in Kingsplot and you'll be expected to go," Millie spoke up. "You can't just spend your days roaming the mansion."

That was exactly what I wanted to do.

"Show him to his room," Thomas said to Wane. "Millie will bring him something to eat later."

"I will?" Millie complained, sounding like an older version of Wane. "Why not? Send the aged woman up the stairs."

They obviously needed to get together to work out who did what to me when. Thomas and Millie began to argue about age and responsibility while Wane grabbed my suitcase and began to walk away. It seemed like a good idea to follow her. We stepped through the hall and into what looked to be another kitchen. This kitchen however was cold and dead, as if no one had cooked anything in it in sometime. Once through the second kitchen, we entered a wide foyer with stairs that climbed up both sides of the walls.

"This isn't the main floor," Wane said informatively. "This floor has the kitchens and the servant's quarters."

The walls and ceilings were ornate and rich looking, but the rest of the floor was empty. There were no chairs or pictures or decorations of any kind. I figured it was because it was the servant's floor, but as we ascended the stairs to the main floor I could see that it too was incredibly bare and void of furniture. I wished Mr. Claude had had the sense to pack my skateboard so I could skate around the house.

"It seems empty," I said.

"Your uncle has sold many of the furnishings," Wane said.

"It looks like he sold them all," I said innocently.

"I wouldn't mention that to him," she said. "He's touchy about it. This is the main floor. You're welcome to spend time here, but I suggest that if a door is locked you leave it be."

It was such a stupid thing to say to a bored fifteen-year-old.

"Come on," she insisted.

We climbed another set of stairs, this one incredibly more lavish than the last. The rail was covered with intricately carved leaves and branches and the edge of each step was gold. The stairs took us to the third floor. I was surprised to see a few pieces of furniture hulking under dusty white sheets.

The entire house was gloomy and dark. The only light came from the hundreds of undressed windows along the walls. I couldn't see a lamp anywhere.

I followed Wane down a mustard-colored hall to a large bedroom that faced the front of the house. The front corner room had large windows on two of its walls. A big, fancy, high bed stood against the back wall and two thick rugs lay on the wood floor. Near one window sat a soft-looking chair and a small, square table with a lamp on it. I could also see two closet doors.

"This is your room," Wane said kindly, setting down my suitcase by the door. "Kinda lonely, but it should stay warm enough. There's a bathroom right across the hall."

"Who else lives on this floor?" I asked nervously.

"No one."

"Just me?" I panicked bravely, not exactly comfortable with occupying an entire creepy floor by myself. "Where's my uncle?"

Wane looked around cautiously and then closed the door, trapping both of us in the room.

"Listen," she whispered. "I know from what Millie's been telling me that you've had a bit of a rough spot but there are a few things you should be careful of while you're here. Your uncle will call for you when he wants to. Understand? He's best not bothered. Lately he seems even more confused than usual. You're welcome to wander the house, but the top floor is off limits. Your uncle resides above it in the dome, and he doesn't like surprises. Also, as I've said, leave locked doors locked. You'll be perfectly safe right here. Millie will bring you food and collect your laundry and Thomas will take you where you need to go. You can spend time outside, but there's no going behind the mansion. Understand?"

"Why?" I had to ask.

"There's nothing back there but unmanaged landscape," Wane answered. "Scott, the gardener, can barely keep up with the front. You could hurt yourself or get lost."

"Lost?" I laughed.

"Your uncle's property goes on for miles," Wane said

harshly. "There have been more than a couple of people who have wandered off and never made it back."

"You're kidding?"

Wane looked at me in such a way that I no longer doubted her sincerity.

"Is there a TV?" I asked, looking around the sparse room.

"No," she said quickly.

"No TV?" I asked, as panicked about that as having to stay here alone.

"I'll see if I can find you one," Wane said sympathetically. "There's probably one somewhere in this drafty house. Until then I'll bring you some books."

"And a dictionary?"

Wane smiled and nodded.

"Oh, and a skateboard."

Wane tilted her head and scrunched her face. "I'll see what I can do," she finally said.

"Thanks," I said.

I moved my suitcase to the bed and looked out the front window. The outdoors were still wet and green.

"Beck," Wane said softly. "I'm sorry for your situation, but we're glad you're here. It will be nice to have a little life back in this house. I know we can't replace your mother, but we love your uncle and feel as if we're all family. So, if I can help, just pull the bell rope hanging by your bed. I might not come instantly, but I'll make my way here as soon as possible."

"Is there a phone?"

"In the kitchen," she answered. "Do you need to call some-one?"

I thought about it a second and realized that I had absolutely no one to call.

Wane looked around the room and tried to smile a comforting smile. "You going to be okay?"

I nodded my head, wondering how in the world I could ever find enough words to express how uncomfortable and un-okay I actually was.

"Good," Wane said, opening up the door. "Welcome to the house of Phillips. Thomas will take you to school tomorrow morning. I'm sure gaining a few friends will make things easier."

Wane exited the room, closing the door behind her. I sat on the bed and put my head in my hands. The black T-shirt I was wearing expressed my feelings perfectly.

I had never felt so alone.

In the year 1828 everything changed for Edward. The government decided Edward had not been paying enough taxes. Edward fought the charges, making those in control angry. Eventually, they took everything from him—his home, his land, and almost every coin he had ever earned. Edward's wife went crazy, taking their two daughters and leaving him. Edward moved to the Isle of Man in the middle of the Irish Sea with Bruno, where they found a small plot of land to farm. He was bitter, angry, and poor.

Excerpt from section three of The Grim Knot, *as recorded by Daniel Phillips*

CHAPTER 5

Tonight I Am Aware

DON'T GET ME WRONG, I WAS still completely uneasy, but more than that, I was bored. No TV, no computer, nothing. Millie had brought me some delicious food at about five o'clock—half a roasted chicken, orange-flavored rolls, some green things I'd never seen before, and mashed potatoes so buttery and soft I was tempted to rub them on my face—but now the only thing occupying my time was digestion.

I had already unpacked my things and even straightened my closet, pretending I actually cared about the few clothes I had. I changed out of my black T-shirt into a red one thinking it might make my life less dark.

Nope.

I looked in the large mirror next to my closet and ran my

hands through my long brown hair. My ears poked out and made me think of Thomas.

"I gotta get out of here," I whispered to myself.

I opened my door and stepped out into the hall. With the sun going down, the entire floor was quickly filling with dark shadows.

"Hello?" I called softly, my voice creating a dull, haunting echo.

I looked across the hall at the bathroom. I had been there earlier and thought it was the biggest bathroom I had ever seen. It had taken forever to bring up any sort of warm water.

The large empty hallway of the mansion rattled in spots and moaned in others as the wind moved around outside and through the cracks in the walls. I reached for the light switch on the wall, but it didn't work. It seemed the only electricity on the entire floor was in my bedroom and bathroom. It wasn't a comforting thought.

I took a flight of stairs going up and came out on the fourth floor where there was a giant room whose walls were lined with massive floor-to-ceiling mirrors. The fading daylight reflected nicely against the glass and made the place sparkle.

Somewhere very far away, and perhaps a few floors down, a door slammed. I quickly crossed the mammoth mirrored room, exiting along another lengthy hallway. I thought about leaving breadcrumbs or some sort of trail so I could make it back, but I had no bread or pebbles on me. I tried opening a few doors, but most of them were locked. The doors that did open only exposed empty rooms and dusty closets.

I took the stairs to the fifth floor. There were a few more pieces of furniture on this floor and tons of rooms. As with the other floors almost half the doors were locked. It would take a long time to check every one of them.

The sixth floor had even more furniture than the fifth floor. Most of the windows had drapes, and there were lamps on the tables and pillows on the hard, formal-looking couches. I found another set of stairs, but the door at the top was locked.

"Stupid door," I said, bothered that it was blocking my progress.

As I descended the stairs and walked across the sixth floor, it struck me that the only windows I had seen were the ones facing the front of the estate. In the larger rooms there were no windows, only large mirrors covering the openings instead. I noticed too that all the locked doors belonged to rooms that faced the back of the house.

I knew I could not go to bed until I had gotten at least one glimpse of the back of the house. I ran down the next set of stairs, feeling the diminishing light of day chasing me. I got to my floor and made my way down to the next. The bare floor was easy to jog across. I jumped down another set of stairs.

The first floor was dark, but there were a few lights glimmering in the hallway. I couldn't see anyone around. I found a door that lead out the side of the mansion, so I exited.

My feet scraped across the stone walkway as I walked back along the side of the house. At the front corner of the mansion there was a wall of tall, thick shrubbery at least fifteen feet tall. It extended past the house as far as I could see. I tried to push through the branches, but the hedge was too dense to even reach through.

I walked along the tall shrubbery, looking for any sort of entrance or gap. The sun was down and the mist-filled air made my hair wet and cold. I turned to go back inside the house, but stopped, taking a stronger look at the bush. I wanted to see what was beyond the bush more than anything. As I gazed at the shrubbery, the short branches sank inward, creating a depression in the foliage.

I rubbed my eyes, certain I was seeing things. I wasn't. The depression was still there. I touched the bush. The leaves and branches closest to my fingers curled back like the wicked witch's pointed shoes after her wicked sister reached for them. I pulled my hand away and the shrub filled itself in. I reached out again, but this time nothing happened.

"Are you okay?" a voice said.

I turned around quickly, my heart beating as fast as my mind was racing. I had not expected to hear anyone and I felt like I had been caught doing something I shouldn't be.

"Who's there?" I asked the dark air.

"You the relative?" the voice asked.

I tried to see who was talking to me, but thanks to the wind, I couldn't even discern the direction the voice was coming from.

"Over here," the voice called.

I spun around once more to see a boy drop down from the trees on the other side of the lane. He stood up and approached me. He was a short kid with big green eyes and wide shoulders. He had curly black hair and flat ears. His legs looked as long as his arms, and he was smiling in a way that normally I would have made fun of. However, seeing as how he had just dropped from a tree, and I had no idea who he was, or if he was trouble, I decided not to give him a hard time just yet.

"Who are you?" I asked.

"Milo," he answered authoritatively. "Milo Flann. You the loon's offspring?"

"By *loon*, do you mean my *uncle*?" I said irritated.

"Hold on," Milo said, showing me his palms. "I didn't mean to give you grief. Have you met him?"

"My uncle?" I asked.

Milo nodded.

"Not yet," I admitted.

"Well, if after you meet him, you don't think he's a loon, I'll apologize."

"That bad?"

"Not many people speak fondly of him," Milo said. "I've heard all kinds of stories in the short time I've been here."

"He let me come live here," I said defensively.

"He had nothing to do with that," Milo scoffed. "He probably doesn't even know you're here. Thomas and Millie are the ones who let you come."

"How do you know that?"

"Well, I know it sure wasn't your uncle," Milo said. "And it certainly wasn't me. So, do you have a name?"

"Beck."

"Like Becky?"

I instinctively made a fist. "Yeah, exactly like Becky," I said sarcastically, having heard that one a million times before.

"Oh," was Milo's only reply.

Wind moved moisture through the air like weak sprinklers. I looked at the huge manor and started to worry about ever finding my way to my room again.

"I should probably go in," I said.

"Why?" Milo asked. "Is someone waiting for you?"

"No," I said, realizing that there was nobody waiting for me anywhere. "I wanna explore the house."

"That could take you years," Milo said, his curly black hair bouncing softly as he talked. "How many floors are there? It's hard to tell from out here."

"Seven," I answered. "But I can't go higher than the sixth because all the doors are locked. My uncle lives in the top dome with the copper roof."

"Sometimes he has a light on and you can see him pacing," Milo said.

I looked up at the top of the manor. The dome was unlit.

"So the manor has seven floors and a basement?" Milo asked reflectively.

"What basement?" I asked, glancing back in the direction of the mansion. It was dark enough now that I couldn't see it clearly from so far away. "There's no basement."

"Anymore," Milo said casually, holding onto a nearby tree like a monkey.

"What's that supposed to mean?" I asked, confused.

"I don't know," Milo said. "I just heard that years ago your uncle had the entire basement filled in with dirt."

"Why would he do that?"

"Like I said, Beck, he's a loon." Milo smiled. "No offense. It's fun to watch him pace back and forth, talking to himself. Maybe he filled in the basement just for crazy's sake."

Now I wanted to see if there really was a basement as much as I wanted to see what was back behind the house in the forest.

"Have you been to the backyard?" I asked.

"Of course," Milo bragged. "I live at the edge of the forest."

"Why doesn't anyone want me back there?" I asked.

"Probably because it's a mess," Milo said. "Or maybe there's something secret hidden there. If you want, I'd be happy to take you there tomorrow after school."

"That'd be great," I said honestly. "Are there any other kids around here?"

"Not really," Milo said. "The Figgins family lives nearby and they have a girl about our age. There are also a couple of kids not too far down the mountain. But most everyone lives just outside of Kingsplot or right in town."

I tried not to look too disappointed.

"I should go," Milo said. "My family will wonder if the woods have eaten me. I guess I'll see you at school. Nice to meet you, Beck."

"Same to you," I replied.

Milo jumped away as if he were playing a lengthy game of hopscotch. It felt good knowing someone. I wasn't alone. The thought of going to school wasn't quite so painful now that I had met Milo. I hoped he wasn't one of those kids that the rest of the school liked to pick on.

The wind whistled through the trees and shrubs, sounding as if Mother Nature was taking a long drink through a thin straw.

I touched the shrubbery again, wondering if I could make it move again. Nothing happened. I thought of what Milo had said about a basement and turned back to the house. The sky was black and only three windows in the entire mansion were lit up.

When I reached the mansion there was no sign of a basement. The dirt and flowerbeds rested right up against the mansion with no visible basement windows or doors showing. The soil did slant up toward the house a bit, but it looked to me like there was nothing but a foundation.

"You can't bury a basement," I laughed.

I went inside and worked my way through the maze of halls and rooms until I found the kitchen. Millie was cleaning pots by herself. She noticed me and tried to smile.

"Can I help?" I asked, accustomed to doing all the dishes when my mother was alive.

"Certainly not," she said. "I know my place."

"The food was great," I tried.

Millie grunted.

"What was that green stuff?"

"Brussels sprouts and butter," she said, still scrubbing.

"I've never seen those before."

"You should be in your room, Beck," Millie pointed out. "Thomas will lock up soon and it's best for you to be where you belong."

"Sorry," I said.

Millie sighed and opened a small wooden cupboard near her shoulders. She pulled out a jar of cookies and offered me one.

I took one, wondering how old they were.

"I'm not used to having children about," she apologized. "But it's probably wise for you to return to your room."

I hopped down off my stool, chewing the dry cookie. Millie picked up her clean pot and shuffled to put it away. I couldn't help myself.

"Is there a basement?" I asked.

Millie dropped her pot, and the clang rang loudly throughout the entire first floor. She turned to stare me down. "What?"

"I was just wondering if there was a basement," I repeated lamely.

"Do you see a basement?" she asked accusingly.

"No, but—"

"Who has been talking about a basement?" she asked, stepping closer to me and pushing her old face closer to mine.

"A kid I met in the yard—Milo."

"That child is nothing but trouble," she said.

"I didn't think we had a basement."

"Of course not." Millie smiled. "Why don't you take the rest of those cookies to your room?"

I grabbed the cookies.

"Sleep well."

"I wish I could sleep on the same floor as everyone else," I said.

"There's an order to things," she insisted, zero sympathy in her voice or inflection. "Goodnight, Mr. Phillips."

"Beck," I corrected her.

"Beck." She smiled.

I shuffled off slowly to my deserted floor and wondered if the home I now lived in really had a basement. And if it did, why would anyone want to hide it?

I turned on both lights in my room and sat on the edge of the bed, facing the door. I didn't enjoy being alone in such a huge house. I felt like I needed to be ready for anything that might pounce through the door. I stared at my doorknob. It looked like all those on the other doors in the manor—large and brass with what appeared to be a sunflower on the knob. Below the knob was some kind of creature—a dragon, maybe. The keyhole was actually the creature's mouth.

I listened to the wind rattle through the drafty old house and missed the cramped but contained apartment my mother and I had last lived in. I thought about Milo, and Wane, and Kate.

I liked the last thought the best. I began to envision scenarios where I might run into her and she would wrap her arms around me and go on and on about how happy she was to see me again. As I thought of Kate, it hit me fully that this was my new home. I wasn't here to visit, or for an extended vacation—I was here to live. I felt more invisible than I ever had; a single fish swimming in an ocean-sized home. I couldn't imagine anyone even realizing I was here. Or caring.

"Thanks a lot, Mom," I sighed.

The wind howled, and without me even realizing it, sleep pounced on me and put me out.

After three months of dwelling on the Isle of Man, Edward and Bruno received a visitor—an old peddler who was making his way across the Isle. He was a magician and offered to sell them magic in exchange for something to eat. Though the peddler was very hungry, Edward, cruel as ever, gave the peddler a stone to eat.

Excerpt from section three of The Grim Knot, *as recorded by Daniel Phillips*

CHAPTER 6

The Headmaster Routine

I COULDN'T REMEMBER FALLING ASLEEP, but I was painfully aware of waking up. The stupid bell on my wall rang and rang until I got up and yanked on the rope next to it.

"I'm up!" I screamed to nobody.

My eyelids felt like sticky pieces of clay that I had to struggle to pull open. A wet gray light dripped through the windows and spotted the floor of my room. For the first time in my life, I wished I had a vase full of flowers or a colorful painting to break up the blah.

I walked to the front window and looked down to see Thomas talking to a short stocky man with a thick black beard and wiry hair. The stocky man held a rake in his gloved hands. They were talking calmly, but I couldn't hear what they were saying.

I left the window and grabbed some clothes to wear. All I really had were T-shirts and jeans, so I grabbed a green T-shirt and blue jeans and darted across the hallway to the bathroom. A pile of thick, soft towels were stacked near the sink. There was also a new bar of soap and bottle of shampoo sitting on the shower rack. Near the sink was a small bottle of tooth powder.

"Tooth powder?" I said, confused.

I got out my toothbrush and dumped a big shake of tooth powder on the bristles. It was one of the single worst teeth brushings I had ever endured. My mouth foamed up like a rabid dog's.

I showered, got dressed, and then made my way downstairs. Millie was in the kitchen talking to Wane.

"Good morning," Wane said, her short hair damp from being outdoors.

"Morning," I replied.

"I hope you like eggs," Millie said. "We've chickens and they won't stop producing."

"I like eggs," I said, wishing my stomach wasn't as nervous as it was.

Wane smiled. "Was everything all right with your room?" she asked.

"Yes," I answered. "Although I'm not sure I like tooth powder."

"Thomas bought you tooth powder?" Wane asked with surprise. "Millie?"

"Don't look at me," she said. "Thomas thought that's what kids liked."

"In the 1920s," Wane said, shaking her head. "I'll get you some real toothpaste," she said to me.

"Thanks. So what time does school start?" I asked.

"The bus comes in twenty minutes," Millie said.

"Bus? I thought Thomas was taking me."

"Turns out a bus comes this far," Millie shrugged.

"But it's my first day," I said, knowing that I had handled more than my fair share of first days alone before.

"Your taking the bus will save Thomas a number of hours," Wane said.

"Oh, good," I replied sarcastically, wondering what Thomas would do with all that extra time. Maybe he would clean his ears, or work on his stiff posture.

The breakfast Millie made was delicious. I had two biscuits the size of soccer balls smothered in thick white gravy with large bits of sausage. Millie had also made me two scrambled eggs that were fluffier and tastier than any eggs I had ever eaten before. I dipped bits of egg in the gravy and then put spoonfuls of hash browns and gravy-eggs onto slices of soft, toasted bread.

"You're a great cook," I said with a full mouth.

Millie liked that, scooping more gravy onto my plate.

"I used to cook for many people every meal," she bragged.

"Where?" I asked.

Millie looked at Wane and then back at me. "Here," she said.

"So a lot of people lived here?"

"Most lived and worked here," Millie said. "But it's expensive to keep a full staff employed. Now finish up."

After breakfast Thomas drove me to the end of our driveway to wait for the bus. I could have walked it, but Thomas felt the exertion would make me too tired to study properly. I hated to inform him that I most likely wouldn't study properly anyway, but I wanted the ride so I kept quiet.

Outside the mansion's gate, Thomas stopped and pointed to the spot where I should wait.

"The bus will be here in a couple of minutes."

"Is there anyone at the school I should talk to first?" I asked.

"They know you're coming."

I got out of the car and Thomas rolled down his window. "A few people may talk," he said. "But you are a Phillips and should be above it all. Don't pay their words much mind."

"Okay," I said, confused. "What—"

Thomas rolled up his window, turned the car around, and drove back to the mansion.

"Have a nice day," I said sarcastically.

The air was still gray and wet, but there were bits of blue sky in the far distance. From my vantage point, I could see the entire Hagen Valley. The town looked like small black-and-white bits stitched into a fuzzy blanket of green. There were a couple of church spires and I could see the train track running off between the mountains. Thin rays of sunlight pushed down in tight, bright streams. I wished I was standing beneath one of the rays. I loved the beautiful woods and mountains, but I missed the familiarity of the West and the large buckets of sunshine.

I heard the bus engine coughing like a plane struggling to take off. I couldn't actually see it until it turned the last bend and pulled into view. The bus stopped directly in front of me, its exhaust pipe belching out smoke. The door opened and a fat woman who was squeezed in behind the steering wheel smiled at me.

"Come on," she waved. "We've got a schedule. Welcome."

"Thanks," I said, stepping up.

The driver took out a clipboard and looked at the spread-sheet on it.

"Beck Phillips?" she asked.

"Yes."

"Take any seat you wish."

There were only two other kids on the bus. One was Milo, and across the aisle from him was Kate. She wore her long red hair tied back with a black ribbon. Her blue eyes were big and sparkled under the dull light of day. It wasn't exactly how I had imagined running into her, but I decided to go with it.

"Hey, Kate," I said nicely as I walked toward them both in the back. I kept my arms hanging by my side in case she decided to stand up and hug me.

"Well, if it isn't Nancy Drew," she smiled.

This was not going as I had foolishly dreamed. I thought about jumping out of the bus window.

"You know her?" Milo asked me.

"We met on the train," Kate answered coolly. "He was investigating the Case of the Missing Passengers."

"Missing passengers?" Milo said.

"Don't ask," Kate waved.

"Well, it's nice to see you too," I said, taking the seat next to Milo.

"I didn't realize you were one of *them*," she said.

"One of them?" I asked.

Kate shrugged, bored. "My family isn't exactly big on your family," she finally answered.

"What's wrong with my family?" I questioned. "I mean, I still haven't met my uncle."

"He squelched on a deal," Kate said. "He sold my father a

big chunk of land and a lodge and then took back more than half the land. I'm surprised he let us keep the lodge."

"Sorry," I tried.

The bus stopped and two more kids got on. Both of the boys waved at Kate and then sat down a few rows up from us. At the next stop, a girl about Kate's age with none of Kate's beauty got on the bus.

"Nervous?" Milo asked me.

"A bit," I said.

"Don't be. I've only been here a short while myself and it's not too bad," Milo said. "Are you a good student?"

"Depends."

Milo liked that, laughing harder than I thought necessary and hitting me on the shoulder. Kate simply stared out the window. It was a pose I had seen her execute many times on the train.

The bus wound down through the tunnels, filling up with students of all shapes and sizes, and eventually pulling into the town of Kingsplot. I was happy to have a seat near Milo and at least know someone.

The bus passed through a large brick gateway and circled around a roundabout. We veered to the right, coming to a stop in front of a large, ornate building. The school looked older than time and was made of at least a million square stones. Over the front door were two smiling gargoyles and a couple of words in Latin.

"What do the words mean?" I asked Milo, pointing.

"Who knows," he answered. " 'Prepare to be bored'? 'Education hurts'?"

"What's the deal with all the gargoyles around here?"

"Adds character," Milo said. "Now follow me. You'll be in my rotation of classes."

I followed Milo, looking at all the other kids. We walked across an enormous brick courtyard and through the side doors. Everyone looked like they had just stumbled out of a Gap ad. Nobody smiled at me.

I wore a sneer and tried to fit in as best as possible. A number of the male students wore suit jackets and all the girls wore skirts.

"Is there a dress code?" I asked Milo, realizing that he too had on a blazer.

"Yes," he replied.

"Great. Thomas gets me tooth powder, but forgets this?"

"I'm sure they'll let you slide, seeing how it's your first day."

The inside of the school was stone with large banners stretched across the walls and lights that hung down from the center of the ceiling. All the windows were up above the lockers that had obviously been installed many years after the original building had been built. Outside the high windows I could see gray sky and persistent ivy that clung to the building.

"Come on," Milo said, his long arm waving at me to move faster.

I bumped shoulders with a number of students in the hall. I was happy that everyone looked about my height or shorter. I towered over quite a few of the younger kids.

"In here," Milo called.

I followed Milo into a large classroom with ten rows of stadium-style seats with ten seats across each row. At the front of the room was an old desk with a blackboard standing behind it. The ceiling was high and the thin windows located around the room's ceiling made it feel like a cave with skylights.

Students flowed in like reluctant sludge, their body language making it clear that most of them did not want to be here. In a few minutes, the seats were filled and a shrill bell rang.

I sat down next to Milo, hoping not to stand out.

A bitter-looking man with thick hair and an uptight walk stepped stiffly to the front of the room. He wore a high-buttoned shirt with a thin tie and a tweed jacket. The creases on his pants were as straight and ridged as I figured his personality must be. He had bushy eyebrows and a small button nose that was slightly off center of his face. One of his eyebrows was higher than the other, giving him a constant look of suspicion. He looked familiar to me somehow.

He held up his right hand and the class quieted. He then put his attaché case on the desk and pulled out a thin notebook. He flipped it open, sniffed loud enough for us all to hear, and then wrote the word *fortune* on the blackboard.

When he turned his attention back to the class, he noticed me. I might have been imagining, but I could have sworn I saw the color drain from his face.

"You," he said. "Fifth row. And apparently above our dress code."

I squirmed in my seat.

"He's new, Mr. Squall," Milo said.

"Funny," he said. "He looks at least fifteen years worn."

Most of the class laughed politely. A stocky kid with long black hair yelled, "Newbie!"

"Stand and tell us who you are," Mr. Squall insisted, making no effort to stop the taunting.

I stood and felt every eye fall on me.

"I'm Beck Phillips," I said. "I just moved here."

"Phillips?" he asked, surprised. There was a long, awkward pause before he continued. "As in *Aeron* Phillips?"

I nodded.

"Impossible," he whispered.

I couldn't tell for sure, but it looked like there was steam coming out of his ears.

"Did no one mention the dress code?" he finally hissed.

I shook my head.

"Ignorance is a sorry excuse. Come."

Mr. Squall beckoned me toward him impatiently. I moved out of my aisle and down the steps to his desk. He pulled a large wad of wrinkled fabric from his bottom desk drawer. He shook it out with one hand, revealing its true form: a long, blue sports coat.

"Let's have you wear this."

"Excuse me?"

The class laughed impolitely.

"This is the coat of justice," he said smartly, as if he had created something dazzlingly clever. "It helps remind those who need reminding that Callowbrow is a school of organization and obedience. I expect you to wear this coat until you have a proper substitution."

I took the jacket from him and turned it around. It was wrinkled and filthy and had obviously not been laundered in years.

"Really?" I asked as the class snickered. The dark-haired kid said something about owning a jacket just like that before his father had a job.

Mr. Squall shook his head as seriously as if this were an inquisition and a person's life was in the balance.

"The jacket," he insisted.

I put the jacket on. It was at least five sizes too big for me. I couldn't imagine it fitting anyone in Callowbrow properly. It smelled like the back of my old apartment complex on trash day.

"Have a seat," Mr. Squall said. "Ticktock, we're wasting precious time."

I sat down while he gave the rest of the class a brief bio of me.

"Mr. Phillips here is related to Aeron Phillips," he said bitterly. "Aeron currently owns the monstrous and ill-kept estate at the top of the mountains. I say currently, because if what I hear is true, Aeron is having financial difficulties. It'd be a pity for him to lose the mansion, seeing how the Phillips' ancestors founded this valley. But mismanagement and dementia are a terrible combination—hard to balance the books with a half-rotten brain. I personally have never met a man more anxious to meddle in other people's affairs."

I had no idea what Mr. Squall was talking about. My only hope was that none of the other students understood him either.

"Now, to the lesson at hand," he continued.

Mr. Squall turned and circled the word *fortune* on the

chalkboard. He then spent the next hour telling us how too much money made people evil and how greed was a more powerful force than love. He used my uncle and his mistakes as the bad example as often as he could. By the time class was over, I felt as if I had been emotionally beat up.

"Nice guy," I said to Milo once we were in the hall.

"Yeah, he's a real horse's—"

Milo stopped talking. A small cluster of boys was blocking the hallway. The boy at the front of the crowd was the same black-haired boy who had taunted me in class.

"Hey, *Bland*," he mocked, making fun of Milo's last name.

"It's Flann, Wyatt," Milo replied.

"Not from where I'm standing." He laughed. "So, the new kid isn't the newest kid anymore. You got yourself a little friend."

Milo was silent. I sighed, realizing that Milo was indeed one of those kids who was easy to pick on.

I stepped in front of Milo and motioned as if to move through the roadblock. I had dealt with plenty of bullies in my life and I wasn't about to give this kid the satisfaction of bothering me.

"Ladies," I said sarcastically, trying to get past.

"Excuse me?" Wyatt snipped.

"Come on, Milo," I said casually. "We've got to go."

"So, Beck," Wyatt sneered. "How's your daft uncle?"

I decided to at least give the silent treatment a try. Wyatt, on the other hand, wouldn't hear of it.

"Is it true, Beck?" he asked cruelly.

"Yes," I replied seriously, having quickly realized that silence wasn't going to work. "It's true—apparently garbage does have more personality than you. But don't freak out, you beat the garbage soundly in the stench department."

Wyatt looked both confused and upset.

"Listen, Beck," he said, poking me in the chest. "My father has more money than your entire family combined."

"Tell him congratulations from me," I said cheerfully, slapping Wyatt on the shoulder.

Milo stepped back. I could see he was scared, but there was also a look of admiration in his eyes. I liked it. There weren't too many moments in my life when I had been admired. I suppose I should have shown more restraint or just kept my mouth closed, but my personality had never stood for it. I remember being a nine-year-old kid and telling off some teenager who was picking on another teenager. I had a poor sense of how scared I really should be when dealing with other people.

"How's your mother?" Wyatt asked cruelly.

I gazed at him. I could feel redness trying to creep up my

neck. I fought the pigment in my own skin and took a long, soft breath.

"She's dead," I said confidently. "But I have a feeling you knew that. Oh, and my father left us when I was one or two. Hard to say for sure exactly when he left seeing how I was so young and my mother was kind of—what's the word you used?—daft."

I had always found the truth to be much more effective than trying to hide from what I was. I was not about to give Wyatt more ammo to use against me.

"Are you crazy?" he asked, confused.

I stepped up to Wyatt and looked him in his pale green eyes. He stared back at me, finally noticing the couple of inches I had on him.

"Whatever," he said. "This school used to have standards."

I was going to say something clever, but Milo grabbed my wrist as if to inform me of the benefits of letting things go.

"Nice to meet you, Wyatt." I smiled insincerely, turning away from him.

"Wait," Wyatt said. "I'm not done talking to you."

I turned to look at him, happy that he wasn't aware of the benefits of letting things go. I was in the mood for a little excitement. I had never done well at school and most of that was because trouble found me at every turn. Now here I was on my first day of another new school and already I had made an enemy. I was almost happy at the prospect of getting my hands dirty.

"We're not done?" I asked, surprised. "I thought you had used up the extent of your vocabulary."

Wyatt didn't scare me. He was shorter and, despite the few extra pounds around his waist, I had a feeling I could take him easily. Unfortunately for me, Wyatt realized that as well.

"Ellis. Carl," he said, red-faced. "Beck here wants to get through."

Wyatt stepped to the side and his two taller and bigger friends moved forward. Ellis towered four inches above me and had a single eyebrow that stretched across his face and into his sideburns. Carl was my height with blond hair and a crooked nose that had probably been shaped by fighting.

"Listen," I said reasonably, not wanting Milo to get hurt. "We're just trying to walk down the hall."

There was a nice-sized gathering of students surrounding us. Most of them had stopped by, hoping for a good fight.

"Be my guest," Ellis said, thumping me on the chest with his large, rubbery hands.

Carl shoved Milo.

I shoved Carl and was preparing to barrel into the dumb thug when I noticed the ivy pushing through the windows above us. The green leaves swung down and dropped like a web right above Wyatt, Ellis, and Carl.

Wyatt raised an arm, preparing to take a swing at Milo, but was stopped by a shot of ivy that wrapped tightly around his wrist.

"What the—?" Wyatt started to say.

I stepped back, not understanding what was going on. I knew my life had taken a turn for the weird, but this was three steps beyond weird.

Large tendrils of ivy draped over all three of them. They pushed and pulled at the growth, but it was useless. Some ivy grabbed Ellis by the ankles and yanked him upside down.

The fearful faces of the crowd of onlookers told me quite clearly that rampaging ivy was not something that normally happened at Callowbrow. Wyatt began to scream like the class full of home-economic girls I had once dropped in on.

Everyone stepped back in amazement and fear.

The ivy jerked all three boys off the ground and, with steady speed, pulled them up to the ceiling and out of the high windows. We could hear all three of them screaming and crying as they disappeared into the great outdoors.

Just like that, they were gone.

Mr. Squall stepped out of his classroom, demanding to know what all the noise was about. We all stood there like frightened mice, most of the girls twisting their hands nervously. A few kids pointed up, but couldn't find the words to explain what had happened.

"What's going on?" Squall barked.

"Some kids . . . sort of . . . climbed out the window," I managed to say.

Squall looked at me and sneered. "Do you think I'm thick?" he said. "Looking to give Aeron something to laugh about? Now, stop making excuses and get to class."

The group dispersed slowly.

Milo and I made our way to our next class in silence. Our English teacher was a squat woman with a long head and bristle-short hair. She wore a dark navy dress that was too long for her. High on the chalkboard's right corner the name "Professor Phister" was written in blue chalk.

"What was all that?" I asked as I took a seat next to Milo.

"I have no idea," Milo whispered excitedly.

"Do plants usually do that here?"

Milo shrugged. "I haven't been here that long, so maybe. But I've never seen something like that before." Milo shook his head in disbelief. "Should we tell someone about Wyatt?" he asked. "They could be hurt."

His concern for Wyatt and his friends ended as quickly as it had begun. At that moment Wyatt, Ellis, and Carl walked into class, late and covered with dirt and leaves.

"A minute late is still late," Professor Phister scolded. "And the reason for your tardiness?"

Wyatt looked around. No one would make eye contact with him except me.

"We fell into the bushes," he lied angrily, his gaze locked with mine.

"And there was a bunch of spiders in the ivy." Ellis shivered.

"Sit," Professor Phister said impatiently.

They sat, and the rest of the day transpired in a rather normal fashion. Although to be honest, I could not, no matter how I tried, get out of my mind the image of that ivy sneaking through the window and snatching Wyatt and his friends.

There was something significantly different about the town of Kingsplot.

The peddler took the stone and, in a fit of rage, cursed it and the man who had given it to him. He threw the stone into a cave and left the Isle, having no real idea of the impact of his actions. The following night, the village farmhouse burned down and only Bruno escaped alive. Two days later, while digging through the rubble, he found the rock the magician had cursed. The stone glowed as Bruno held it. It was heavy, and when he set it down, the stone would cool and appear to look like any other rock.

Excerpt from section three of The Grim Knot, *as recorded by Daniel Phillips*

CHAPTER 7

A Rush and a Push

MILLIE WAS IN THE KITCHEN creating smells that would make anyone with working nostrils hungry. As usual, she tried to smile at me, but she was more comfortable talking while staring into a bowl or chopping carrots.

"It smells," I said.

"Foul or favorable?"

"Very favorable." I smacked my lips together.

"Good. It's nice to have someone who appreciates food in the house," she said, her good eye looking straight at me.

"What are you making?"

"Not sure yet," Millie admitted. "The beginnings of dinner."

"I still haven't met my uncle," I pointed out.

"You will. Don't rush what you don't understand."

I hated the way adults spoke.

I looked at the clock. "Where's Wane?" I asked, wanting to know where everyone was before I snuck into the woods behind the house.

"She's at the stables."

"Are there any horses?"

"Only a few," Millie said sadly. "There used to be stables full of handsome stallions."

"And Thomas?"

"He's not exactly handsome," Millie said absentmindedly.

"I mean where is he?"

"Shopping in town." Millie blushed. "Your school called and informed us of your need for a jacket. He's picking up one for you."

"Thanks," I said, not exactly sure how I felt about Thomas picking out my clothes.

Millie handed me a piece of bread as thick as half a normal loaf and covered in red jam. A perfectly square piece of butter melted slowly in the middle of it.

"Thank you," I smiled.

I stood up and moved to the outside door that led to the courtyard.

"Where are you going?" Millie asked suspiciously.

"Just outside," I said. "I thought I'd eat and walk. Maybe I'll go down to the road."

"Stay forward of the house," she insisted. "I don't want you getting hurt or turning up lost."

I took a huge bite of bread and jam. It was so warm and delicious, the flavor almost stunned me. I forced my feet to work and stepped out of the kitchen into the hall and back outside.

The sky was predictably gray. A triangle of thick mist moved slowly through the air and smeared itself up against the mansion's stone wall. The poorly manicured bushes that circled the drive shivered in the light wind. I looked up and smiled at the gargoyles gazing down at me.

I finished my bread and then ran as fast as I could along the side of the mansion. I followed the towering hedge past where I had run into Milo the night before and all the way to the edge of the thick forest where it ended abruptly at the base of a giant moss-covered statue shaped like a crouching tiger.

I stopped and caught my breath.

"Don't run much, do you?" Milo observed.

I looked up in a tree, not terribly surprised to see him there. Milo jumped down from the branches and dusted off his palms. We had talked a bit about what had happened at school, but it still confused both of us.

"That was just too weird."

"It was good, though," he said. "Very good."

"I guess. We could have taken them."

"So, have you found the basement yet?"

"No."

"Wanna see the backyard?"

"That's why I'm out here," I said. "Instead of in the kitchen with Millie eating fresh bread."

Milo licked his lips. "Next time bring some for me," he said. "My mom's a lousy cook."

Milo began to walk and I followed. We ducked under some low hanging branches and crossed a small stream that was running strong. A tall rock cliff rose from the ground, forcing us to struggle to climb its back before running quickly over the knoll it created.

The forest was remarkably dense and I could see now how it would be possible for a person to get lost.

Milo turned behind a grove of short trees and we threaded ourselves like string through tons of trees toward the back of the forest. After a couple hundred feet, the thick trees shrank to overgrown bushes. Beyond the bushes grew waist-high grass and wicked-looking shrubbery. I could see tops of stones and little bits of a large fountain sticking up among the growth.

Milo stopped. We stood still, listening to the sound of our hearts slowing and the birds screaming in the distance.

"This is it," Milo said.

I could barely see the back of the mansion from where we were. It looked to be at least a mile away. There was a set of stone steps leading down to a stagnant pond. Thin remains of what must have once been wide walking paths and roads crisscrossed the area, entirely filled in with weeds.

I was disappointed. I had no real idea what I had expected, but more trees and grass was not what I had been hoping for.

"They were right," I said. "This place is an ugly mess."

"That gardener's just lazy," Milo said. "This could be a great place. Like a park or something."

"How far back does it go?" I asked.

"Quite a ways," Milo said. "Back that other direction a good bit is my house. I'd take you there, but my mother's on one today."

"And which direction does Kate live?" I tried to ask casually.

Milo smiled and pointed further to the right. "Don't mess with her. She's colder than dry ice."

I had always thought dry ice was amazing.

"Come on," Milo said, beginning to run.

We ran for a few hundred yards and came to a stop in front of a massive field of stones. I had never seen anything like it. Millions, if not billions of stones of all shapes and sizes ran like a fat river up through one of the mountain's ravines.

"Holy—"

"Shale," Milo said. "Mostly. Have you ever seen so many rocks?"

I shook my head. I couldn't even take it all in. I picked up a rock and threw it out in the middle of the others. Milo did the same and then we turned and walked back into the forest.

"So, what's in that direction?" I asked, pointing further back to where the trees began to reach higher up the mountain slope.

I could see a dark stone wall rising above the ground and a large mass of gray mist hovering over it.

"That's not anything," Milo said. "Just a wall."

"A wall?" I asked, feeling oddly curious.

"Well, like a weird, square wall," Milo said.

"So, there's something in the middle of it?"

"I don't know," Milo admitted. "No one can get inside."

"Isn't there a door?"

"There's like a blocked-in arch," he said. "You can't get in."

That sounded like a challenge.

"I wanna see it," I insisted.

Milo shrugged and followed me as I stepped quickly through the foliage.

"You're going to be disappointed," Milo warned. "My father even tried to find a way in. There's nothing."

Now I knew I had to see the wall. I ran faster, climbing down another set of stairs and running across a wide stretch of land that had probably been an impressive lawn years ago. I jumped through a brick archway that was circling a section of the yard. The bricks at the back of the circle had crumbled, creating an exit.

A gigantic deer bolted in front of me and darted off to the right. The surprise stopped me.

"Did you see that?" I asked.

"This forest is fat with game."

"You talk funny," I said, not sure if Milo was trying to sound proper or like some sort of hip forest thug.

"There are lots of things to shoot," he clarified.

I didn't care at the moment. I ran some more, scaring three birds from bushes and into the air. I could see the stone wall now. It was much larger than it had looked from a distance. As I drew closer, I figured it was at least three stories high. The solid black stone was covered with pits and mold.

I looked up at the wall with awe.

Milo finally caught up.

"See," he panted spastically. "I told you, a wall."

I stepped along the wall, running my hand over its wet, moldy surface.

"It looks hundreds of years old," I said.

"Could be," Milo said. "There are all kinds of weird ruins all over this mountain."

We reached the corner of the wall where it turned at a ninety-degree angle and ran into the trees.

"Come on," I insisted.

I ran along the side, looking for any sign of an opening or entrance. There was not so much as a knob or a crack anywhere. On the back wall, though, was a large archway that had been bricked in. Above the arch in raised black stone was the word Conservatory. The archway looked like it had been closed up many years ago. I pushed against the bricks. They felt more solid than the actual stone.

The fourth side was nothing but black stone. Eventually we made it around the entire thing. The whole conservatory was crowned with thick strings of mist.

"So, what is it?" I asked, out of breath and confused.

"A wall," Milo insisted.

"It's more than a wall," I said. "The back says conservatory. And that bricked-in entrance is maddening."

"Maybe there's a tunnel under one of the walls," Milo said.

"I looked for that. I couldn't see anything."

"Maybe it's just a monument or something," Milo suggested.

Both of us looked up at the towering blackness.

"A monument to what?" I said.

Another giant deer decided that right then was the best moment for it to jump from where it was hiding and scare the life out of me.

"Stupid deer," I said, embarrassed about being startled. "We need a ladder."

"I think they're easier to shoot with a rifle."

"I'm not talking about the deer," I said, hitting Milo on the back of his shoulder. "We need a ladder to look over the wall."

"Or a catapult," Milo said seriously.

"I think a ladder would work better."

"I guess, but I've never seen a ladder that tall."

"What about a tree?" I realized with excitement.

I began to closely look at the surrounding trees. None of them had any low branches. In fact, they all were oddly branch-free with green needles only at the top. I ran around the corner and saw the same deformity on all the trees.

"There's something in there," I whispered.

I walked around the whole conservatory again, checking the walls more carefully. There was nothing but black stone and a bricked-in archway. I considered hiking the mountain behind the forest, but I could tell that it sloped too gradually for me to be able to get above the conservatory and peer in.

"I've gotta get in," I said. "There has to be—"

My thoughts were interrupted by a heavy, gloved hand grabbing my right shoulder. I jumped much higher than when the deer had startled me. I tried to turn, but the hand held me tightly. Milo took off running.

"What are you doing here?" the mouth, attached to the face that was attached to the body that was attached to the hand that held me, asked.

"I was just walking around," I said.

The hand opened and I spun around. The man was older than most dads I had seen, but younger than any grandfathers. He was wearing a knit cap and pants that buttoned just below the knee. His eyes were hooded and dark and, like most of the people I had met at the mansion, it looked as if he hadn't practiced his smile in some time. I recognized him from that morning when I had seen him talking to Thomas below my window. The dirt on his gloves and knees made me think he was most likely Scott, the gardener.

"Just walking around?" he questioned suspiciously. "Didn't Millie and her bunch tell you to stay away from the gardens?"

I wanted to point out that I'd only met three people so far and that technically *a bunch* was more like six or seven.

"Didn't she?"

I nodded guiltily. "I couldn't tell where the front of the yard ended and the back began," I tried, hoping he would just think I was lost.

"See the back of the manor?" he said, spinning me around.

It was far away, but I could definitely see that I was behind the house. The copper-roofed dome on top of the mansion stood out like a sore thumb.

"Is that the house?" I said innocently, holding my hand above my eyes to see. "Wow. I didn't know I had wandered so far. Well, I guess I'll be on my way."

"No, you won't. Come with me," he barked.

For about two seconds I thought about making a run for it, but his gloved hand pulling on my right ear was a powerful persuasion. He dragged me back through the overgrown garden. In between my yelping, I tried to explain to him that I could walk by myself.

He wasn't buying it. He pinched my ear even harder and picked up his pace.

"Foolish kids," he mumbled as he marched through the thorny weeds. "Don't know where to stick your wet noses."

I touched my nose to see if it was wet.

That only made him angrier. He yanked my ear and growled, pulling me up some hidden steps and through an arbor.

"You're going to pull my ear off!" I argued.

"It's not like you listen with it anyhow," he threw back.

He had a pretty good point, and one heck of a grip.

We finally reached the mansion. He dragged me up the stairs, into the hallway, and then pushed me with his knee into the kitchen. Millie looked up in astonishment as I flew against her table and steadied myself. I rubbed my red ear and looked back at the gardener with daggers in my eyes.

"What in the name of Peter is going on?" Millie asked, stepping around the table to see if I was okay. "Scott, you don't go pushing children around."

"Yeah," I said.

"Caught him in the back. Near the . . . at the far rear," Scott said unapologetically. "Far rear."

Millie looked at me with bother in her eyes. "Is that true, Beck?"

"I got lost," I tried again. This time my excuse sounded even lamer.

"He was there with that pesky kid," Scott growled. "Staring at the black wall and up to no good, I imagine."

I decided to strike while I could. "What is that place?"

Scott slammed his palm against the door frame. "You never seen a wall before?" he asked mockingly. "There are miles of earth out in front of the manor. Stay away from the back garden for your own safety. It's dangerous out there."

"It didn't look too dangerous," I argued. "And what's a conservatory?"

It was the wrong thing to say. Even Millie looked angry at
me.

"I don't care if you found slides and Ferris wheels," she
ordered. "You are instructed to stay away from the back gardens.
And stay away from that Milo child while you're at it."

I had never really cared for Ferris wheels, but it felt like an
inappropriate time to confess that.

Scott turned and stormed out triumphantly. Millie went
back to kneading bread, but now she looked more wounded
than bothered.

"Sorry, Millie," I said. "Really, I was just walking around."

"I'll bring your supper up in a bit," was her only reply.

I made my way upstairs thinking only of the conservatory
and how I could possibly get over the wall. There was no way my
personality or mind could simply forget about it.

I wanted in.

With his father gone, Bruno had nothing. His heart was dark with sorrow and filled with hatred for all that had been taken from him and his family. Alone and with no possessions, Bruno began to concentrate on farming. With the pillage gift, his crops grew fast and strong, even among the rocks. Soon he had a small, thriving farm and a tiny home. Every night he would take out the cursed stone and hold it, letting it glow in his hands. The rock reminded him of the unsatisfied vengeance and anger he held in his heart.

Excerpt from section four of The Grim Knot, *as recorded by Daniel Phillips*

CHAPTER 8

I Started Something

DINNER WAS FANTASTIC. I had never before licked my plate clean—twice. Wane still hadn't brought me a TV but she did bring me a dictionary. I was surprised to see just how many words I had been previously unaware of. After looking at the dictionary, I spent some time reading and trying to understand my mother's journal. I counted the number of times she mentioned me directly (twenty-seven) and the number of times she mentioned my father (zero).

Wane had also been kind enough to bring me a picture of my uncle. She knew I was anxious to meet him and thought a picture of him would help prepare me. I held the picture next to the one I had of my mother. There was no question they were related. They both had the same nose, freckles under their eyes, and a milder version of my smile.

I set the pictures down and sprawled out on my bed. The house whistled and purred as the evening winds snaked through the walls. I was happy I had survived my first day at school, but there was another one coming tomorrow. My mind kept replaying the moment Wyatt and his friends had been lifted up by the ivy. It made so little sense that after a few minutes of thinking about it, I almost convinced myself that it had never actually happened.

"I must have seen things wrong," I reasoned.

But then I remembered the shrub I had seen change last night and the walled section of the garden behind the manor.

I fell asleep thinking that perhaps everything I had experienced was just a dream and that in a few minutes I would wake up, tell my mother about it and that would be that.

Four hours later I woke to the sound of wind pounding against my window. Someone had turned off my light. I figured Millie or Wane had come by to collect my dishes and found me sleeping.

I stood up and the wood floor moaned like a sick cow. I reached for the light switch, but when I flipped it, nothing happened.

The wind was relentless. The door to my bedroom popped open and a steady stream of air slipped through. I looked into the hall and saw nothing but darkness. I was ready to close my door and pretend everything was going to be okay, when I saw a small hint of light coming from where the stairs were.

"Wane?" I whispered. "Millie?"

Unless one of them spoke wind, they didn't reply.

"Thomas?"

I walked down the hall to where the stairs began their descent. The little bit of light was almost unnoticeable. I thought maybe I had been seeing things in the dark, but then, at the bottom of the stairs, a dull flash of light flickered.

"Hello?" I called down.

I took the stairs carefully, wishing I had a stick or something to defend myself with.

"Who's there?"

It was pitch black at the bottom of the stairs with no sign of the strange light. I could feel streams of wind blowing around my ankles and past the top of my head. At the far end of the main floor's long hall a pinpoint of weak light glimmered, dancing and winking in the darkness. I was no scientist, but even I knew light wasn't supposed to disappear and then reappear further away.

There was an uneasy chattering in the air—like the wind was trying to warn me of something. As usual I ignored any voice of reason and kept my eyes on the light.

I followed the miniscule trace of light to the first floor. I was in the hall leading to the kitchens. I suspected that Millie and Wane were in bed. Thomas, on the other hand, made it clear he was sleeping by snoring loud enough that I could hear it.

Though I had been on this floor more than any other, I still had probably only explored a fourth of it. I walked away from the staff's quarters to the other half of the manor. The wind pulsated more than it blew. I could feel the pressure of the windows flexing in and out. My heart raised a notch in my throat with each step I took. The wind's pulsation beat thoughts into my head. I could remember every horror movie I had ever seen. I felt like the wide assortment of villains in those movies were now hiding somewhere on this floor, waiting to attack me.

"I'm living this," I whispered to myself, still not completely believing my life at the moment. "Mom, if there's danger down here, let me know."

I figured she hadn't given me much advice while she was alive but maybe in death, with a little more insight and time, she might reach out and steer me the right way.

That didn't appear to be the case.

I could hear the wind chattering in the darkness, and like the sort of idiot I would have scolded for going down a dark hall, I walked right down the dark hall. I would have kept walking if it had not been for a wall stopping my progress. I ran right into it, hitting my nose hard enough for me to swear.

"Sorry, Mom," I said, just in case she was listening.

I felt along the wall, looking for another direction to walk. There wasn't any. I had walked into a dead end where there was a door with a locked handle. A faint light slipped out from under the door and briefly danced across my toes.

Every hair on my neck stood up and then wilted. I put my ear to the door, hoping to hear someone or something moving around on the other side. I could only hear the wind muttering and moaning. I rattled the locked knob, trying to pop the door open.

It was no use. I let go of the knob and watched the light along the bottom of the door fade to black. I would have just turned around, adding tonight's mystery to the growing list of oddities Kingsplot was providing, but then I heard something fiddling with the lock on the other side of the door.

I stepped back, the unexpected sound so surprising and unsettling I could barely keep my knees working. It sounded like tiny hands nervously rattling the lock as the wind continued to mutter. There was a soft, crisp click and then nothing.

Everything in me was telling me to just walk away. Well, not everything, because despite the signals my brain was sending to my feet to move away, the signal my hands were receiving was stronger. I could feel my fingers groping for the doorknob.

I turned the handle again and this time the door pushed

open. I tried to control my breathing, but my throat began doing weird things with the air it was taking in. I couldn't hear anything but my breath.

I gently pushed the door and it swung open all the way. The hinges squeaked lightly as the door came to rest against the wall.

I couldn't see anything.

"Who's there?" I asked.

My breathing was so loud. I felt certain everyone within a ten-mile radius could hear me.

"Someone's there. I heard you," I whispered.

The thin line of light shimmered from under the baseboard on the far wall. As much as I wanted to, I couldn't turn back. I walked across the room.

The light was coming from somewhere behind the wall. I kicked at the baseboard and felt my toes push into a soft spot on the wall. Surprised, I pulled my foot away and saw I'd created a small hole. I kicked again, creating a slightly bigger hole. Light as dull as wet newspaper dripped out slowly. I dropped to my knees and then down on my stomach so I could peer through the hole.

A large earthen tunnel sloped downward. At the bottom of the dirt tunnel there was a bend. Whatever was causing the light was around that turn.

I lay on the floor, gazing into the dimly lit hole. I stuck my fingers in and pulled at the wall. The opening tore easily, creating a tear twice the size of the original hole.

The tunnel was larger than I'd thought.

I was about to tear the hole wide open, when I saw a shadow moving far down in the hole, blocking the light.

I pushed onto my elbows and then my knees in one frantic jump. As I got to my feet, the wind began to chatter even stronger. It was so dark and, even though the night was cool, I felt sweat gathering all over my body.

I ran back across the room. I could barely see the outline of the room's door. There was a key lodged in the keyhole on the inside. I grabbed it and locked the door behind me as quickly as I could.

I stood with my back against the closed door, trying to catch my breath. I heard someone twisting the knob again and decided I had rested long enough. I ran down the hall and back up the stairs to the main floor.

It was dark, but my fear gave me a keen sense of direction. I found the stairs leading to the third floor and sprinted to my room, certain that someone or *something* was right behind me.

I slammed my door shut and reached for the light switch. The electricity was working again. I turned the latch, bolting the door closed, and looked around the room to make sure I really was alone.

It was just me and the jittery wind.

I double checked the lock on my door and then circled my bedroom, kicking at the baseboards to make sure I didn't have any weak walls. Everything was solid. I couldn't decide if I should scream or curl up in a ball and cry.

I didn't like this house.

I didn't want to be here. I wanted to be in a messy apartment making my mom dinner. I wanted to be thinking of ways to bother my classmates, or scrounging for money in my mom's purse to buy a movie ticket.

The wind laughed shrilly at me.

I put my hands over my ears and lay back on my bed. I stayed awake the rest of the night, watching the clock and wondering how I was ever going to live here.

Bruno might very well have been content living forever in the mountains if it had not been for the sickness in his heart. He hated those who had taxed his family into poverty. And he hated even more the peddler who had cursed him.

One evening, while looking at the stone and fanning his hatred like a hot coal, he mistakenly dropped the rock onto a patch of broad-leafed plants. Bruno cursed and told the plants they could have the rotten stone. The plants took him at his word, quickly claiming the rock by wrapping their leaves around it.

Excerpt from section four of The Grim Knot, *as recorded by Daniel Phillips*

CHAPTER 9

Paint an Ugly Picture

Y OU SEEM TIRED," Milo said.

"What gave it away?" I asked sarcastically. "Was it when I fell asleep on the bus and started to drool, or when I fell asleep in Squall's class and started to snore?"

"Sorry," Milo said, hurt. "I was just saying."

"I didn't sleep," I growled as we walked to our lunch table and sat down with our trays.

"Why not?" Milo asked. "Did the gardener tie you up and force you to stay awake?"

"No."

"Millie?"

"No," I said, bothered. "They lectured me, and Scott almost pulled my ear off, but they weren't what kept me up."

"What then?"

It was lunchtime and the cafeteria was a lot more crowded than it had been yesterday. It wasn't because the food was a draw. Today's menu was meatloaf, a square of hard peanut butter, and a salad that looked like a spit-up wad of field greens, mixed with raw baby carrots, and a smear of white dressing running through the whole mess. Milo bragged about how the students had actually helped grow the lettuce in the school garden. I tried to look impressed. I looked around at all the other students who were trying to choke down their meatloaf.

"Seriously," Milo persisted. "Why are you so tired?"

"I guess I can tell you," I whispered. "There's a basement in the manor."

It was Milo's turn to be sarcastic. "Some secret—I told you that a couple of days ago."

"I know, but I didn't believe you."

"So you've seen it?" Milo asked, picking up his peanut butter square and taking a huge bite.

"Yes," I hissed. "And there was someone or something down in it."

"What?" Milo asked enthusiastically.

"Yeah, what?" Wyatt said, walking up to our table. He sat down next to us with his friends on either side of him. "What are you two stumps all excited about? Did they release a new collectable Barbie?"

We both just stared at him.

"You have the stupidest sense of humor," I finally said.

"Shut up," Wyatt said, smashing his palm down on my peanut butter square. "I'm not here to make jokes. I wanna know what you did to us yesterday."

Milo looked nervous.

"I know it was a trick," Wyatt whispered at me. "Who helped you?"

"No one helped me," I said seriously. "The ivy's got my back."

All of us looked up at the windows circling the cafeteria ceiling. I waved as if some of the foliage were signaling me.

"Funny," Wyatt said. "I don't know how you did it, but I'm gonna find out. And when I do—" Wyatt thumped his fist on the table and then pointed at me. "I don't like you."

"Really?" I said, smiling the sort of smile that would make a grandmother give me a cookie, but cause a bully like Wyatt to want to hit me.

"When your family loses your home, my father will buy it up for pennies," Wyatt seethed, stabbing Milo's homegrown salad with a fork. "And from what I've heard, you'd better start packing your bags."

Having been picked on, moved around, disciplined, ignored, bullied, teased, embarrassed, and misunderstood by just about every student and teacher I'd ever known, I was no longer surprised by how cruel and unfriendly people could be. Wyatt's threats and words were similar to half a dozen other kids' who had given me grief over the last few years of my life. There wasn't anything Wyatt could say that would cause me to care. I decided to use one of my favorite tactics in an effort to turn the tables.

"There's a booger on the tip of your nose," I whispered to him, passing a napkin. "You might want to be more careful when you blow."

Wyatt didn't know whether he should take the napkin and clean up, or scream in anger. He did neither. Instead he stomped his feet and pushed Milo's face down into his meatloaf. In doing so, Wyatt helped me discover something that could actually make me care.

I jumped up and knocked Wyatt's right shoulder back with my hand. His two cronies were ready to uneven the odds. Ellis, the single-browed thug, picked up his fork and swung it at me. The tines caught the sleeve of my new jacket and created a long tear. I grabbed my arm and screamed. I could feel small amounts of blood coming from the wound.

Wyatt must have realized the power of the fork because he grabbed his own and took a swing. He missed both of us. His poor aim only made him angrier. He lunged at me and I flipped my tray up, blocking his blow and causing him to push his fist into my uneaten meatloaf. Carl grabbed Milo by the front of his shirt and shoved him backward. I moved to break Milo's fall, but my foot slipped on my spilled milk and I went to the ground on my back.

Wyatt stood over us and smiled. Our actions had attracted the attention of the next table, but no adults. Wyatt lifted his right foot and kicked it toward my stomach. As I moved to block it, flashes of green sprang from across the room like feathery birds.

I heard Ellis scream as more swatches of dark green began to fly around the room. I thought for a second that the ivy was acting up, but I could see from the windows above that the ivy was quiet and still.

Wyatt swatted at the air. I rolled onto my stomach to push myself up and my hand slipped in my spilled salad. As my hand touched the leaves, the entire salad began to scurry across the floor. The leaves leapt into the air and landed on Carl's butt. I watched the lettuce leaves contract and heard Carl scream.

As I stood up, every salad in the room jumped from its cozy section in the lunch trays and flew with fury toward Wyatt and his allies. Wyatt fell backward over a table of students, sliding off the bench and onto the floor.

It seemed like entire heads of lettuce dogpiled him. Wyatt tore at the greenery, screaming and shouting. Ellis and Carl were having similar problems. Ellis took his single brow and ran from the room, covered in lettuce and dressing. Carl swatted at the air and fought violently to scrape the salads off him as a herd of baby carrots climbed his legs.

Students everywhere burst from their seats and ran for cover. A girl with big shoulders fainted, and a boy who had bragged in my math class about not being scared of anything, wilted like a weak flower and crawled under a table to cry.

The few adults in the cafeteria kept yelling for everyone to calm down, but the attacking salads soon convinced them that they had no real control of the situation. Two of the teachers ducked for cover while the third ran out the back door.

"What's happening?" Milo screamed.

"I have no idea!" I screamed back, batting at the air.

Wyatt was still on the ground, rolling like he was on fire and smearing white dressing across the floor. Fleeing students slipped and slid on the dressing, crashing into tables and walls.

"The salads aren't going after anyone but Wyatt and Carl," Milo screamed frantically.

I looked around. Dressing and lettuce was everywhere, but the only people covered in it were Wyatt and Carl. I watched Wyatt spin on the floor, trying desperately to crawl his way out of the cafeteria. Carl was pinned to a table, pleading for his life as tiny carrots worked themselves into his nose and lettuce leaves stuffed themselves into his mouth.

Things looked like they were moving in slow motion. I watched the other students running in fear. I saw Kate hunched down in a corner of the cafeteria, holding a tray over her head and shaking.

Her eyes met mine and the word just came right out of me—"Stop."

Instantly every bit of lettuce shivered and dropped to the floor. Carrots rained down like thick drops of water.

I walked over to Kate and crouched down beside her. "Are you okay?" I asked.

"What was that?" she asked, her eyes wide with fear.

"I have no idea," I answered. "But I think the lettuce had it out for Wyatt. What kind of food are they serving us?"

"Lively food, I guess," Kate said. A small smile appeared on her face and some of the fear left her eyes. I helped her to her feet and her small grin grew a little bigger.

I remembered how much I enjoyed her smile. There were definite perks to heroically saving a damsel in distress.

Milo stepped up to us, wiping a glob of dressing off his sleeve. "How did you stop it?" Milo questioned, seemingly bothered by Kate's closeness to me.

"I just asked," I said, more confused than anyone.

"You asked the lettuce to stop?" Kate smiled nervously. "That's impossible."

I shrugged.

From across the cafeteria, I could hear Wyatt crying and wiping salad off himself. Carl sat up on the table, throwing up buckets of lettuce and shooting carrots out his nose.

I walked over and reached down to pull Wyatt to his feet.

He looked up at me, still crying. "Who *are* you?"

"Here," I said, ignoring his question and keeping my hand extended.

"Get away from me!" Wyatt shouted, knocking my hand aside and standing up on his own. Lettuce slid down him like wet paint. He had dressing all over his face and above his lip like a mustache.

I reached out and picked up a napkin.

"Here," I said sincerely. "You've got something on your nose."

Some people have absolutely no sense of humor. If Wyatt had been holding a bat I'm sure he would have hit me. Instead, he glared at me and motioned for Carl to join him. They stalked out of the cafeteria.

I looked around at the chaos and destruction that remained from the lettuce attacks.

"Remind me to never make you mad," Milo murmured from behind me.

"I think I need help," I said, worried.

Wyatt came back in the cafeteria, flanked by Mr. Squall on one side and Principal Wales on the other. Wyatt pointed at me and the principal motioned for me to come.

"I'm dead," I said.

"Not if there's salad around," Kate said, raising one eyebrow.

I laughed because she was beautiful and I wanted her to like me.

"Nice to see you still have your sense of humor," Milo said in amazement.

I shrugged. "I was beginning to wonder when I would finally get to see the principal's office. I made it all the way to my second day—I think that's a new personal best."

I walked across the cafeteria and followed Principal Wales to his office. My life was following the course it always had. Although I must say, of all the principal's offices I had ever been in his was certainly the stuffiest. It was filled with the most scholarly looking, but in my opinion, useless junk.

"Have a seat," the principal said, trying to stay calm. "Your second day here and already you've caused quite a stir."

I didn't think he was complimenting me, but I said, "Thank you," just in case.

"You have some explaining to do, Mr. Beck."

I smiled. If he was expecting me to clear things up, we were going to be here for a long, long time.

The plants will know what to do. You must simply let them know it is time to grow. They will work for you only so long as you plant what you must. Once the crop is seeded, they will lose all interest in you.

Excerpt from section five of The Grim Knot, *as recorded by Daniel Phillips*

CHAPTER 10

There Is a Glow That Won't Snuff Out

PRINCIPAL WALES LECTURED me for an hour about nothing. He talked about character, integrity, and respect. Luckily for me he had long, rambling stories to go with all of those qualities. When he finally stopped to catch his breath I asked him what it was I had actually done. He stammered and said something about throwing lettuce and causing a commotion.

I asked for proof.

He told me not to be impertinent.

He then warned me if I ever did the thing I had done again, whatever it was that I had done, that I would be in great trouble.

When I got on the bus to go home, everyone grew quiet. The seat next to Milo was filled so I sat by myself in the front row. After most of the students had been dropped off, I worked my way to the back of the bus and sat by Milo. Kate was across the aisle.

"You okay?" Milo asked.

"Sure."

"Everyone's making up their own version of what happened today, Beck," Milo said quietly.

"Good," I said. "Then maybe someone can explain it to me."

"That was so weird, Beck," Kate jumped in, seeming much more interested in me since lunch. "I mean, the lettuce and carrots were moving—by themselves."

I savored the sound of Kate saying my name for a moment before I replied.

"Do things grow differently here?" I asked seriously. "Or do you make lettuce out of something living?"

Kate shook her head. "I can't wrap my mind around an explanation."

"Maybe it's all the moisture in the air," I said. "The things that grow here are just sick of it, or overly confident because of so much water."

"But the salad was dead," she pointed out.

"There must have been enough life left in it," I tried weakly.

"What are you going to tell your uncle?" Milo asked.

"To socialize more," I joked. "I haven't seen my uncle. I'm

not even sure he's up there. Millie could have killed him years ago and now they just have to put on an act."

"Up there?" Kate asked. "Up where?"

"There's a room under the copper dome on the top floor," I explained. "It's such a huge house. When I wander around, I worry I might not make it back to my room."

"And you found the basement last night?" Milo asked.

I nodded.

"Congratulations," Kate smiled. "What—was it hiding under the bottom floor?"

"Funny. It's filled in with dirt," I whispered. "Someone's even moved soil to cover all signs of it from the outside. But I found an entrance behind a wall in one of the rooms. It looks like there's a tunnel leading down. But something was moving—something that unlocked the door for me to get in."

Milo shivered.

"I'm going back tonight," I added, trying to sound brave.

"I wanna go," Kate whispered excitedly. "I get so bored at home. Take me with you."

It was the most enthusiasm I had seen from her. I tried to act cool by shrugging instead of squealing. Apparently Kate was up for adventure.

"Me, too," Milo said.

The bus stopped and the last of the other students got off, leaving just us three and the driver.

"Okay," I said. "If you guys can get out tonight, meet me at two o'clock by the side doors, past the fountain and near the drive."

They both nodded.

"I'll meet you at the end of your drive," Milo said to Kate, "at a quarter to two."

"But listen," I warned. "We have to do it quietly. When I asked Millie about the basement she freaked out. And the tunnel opening is in a room that was locked. I've only been warned about a hundred times by everyone at the house not to mess with locked doors."

"So if we're caught, you're dead," Kate said.

"Exactly."

"I can live with that." She smiled.

"Thanks."

"Should we bring anything?" Milo asked.

"Yeah, a bucket of chicken and some movies," I joked.

"I was just asking," Milo said defensively.

"Sorry, bring a flashlight and a bat or a stick to stab something with," I said, feeling like I was extending a really morbid party invitation.

The bus stopped in front of my drive.

"Two o'clock?" I confirmed.

"Two," they echoed back.

I did my homework, ate dinner in my room, and brushed my teeth with a gnawing nervousness in my gut. I had acted brave on the bus, but when I thought back to how I had felt last night when that shadow had moved behind the wall, I wanted to pack up my things and take the first train away from here.

It was a small comfort to know I wouldn't be going down the tunnel alone, but my gut still ached.

I sat on the edge of my bed and set my alarm clock for 1:50. It was silly of me to even set it seeing as how I couldn't fall asleep. At 1:49 I turned off the alarm and slid out of bed. I got the key from out of my suitcase where I had been hiding it.

I left my room and made my way down the dark hall, feeling the wall for direction. There was no light at all tonight. I wondered if there would be any sign of light behind the wall.

I stepped off the stairs on the bottom floor and listened for sounds of life. Thomas was snoring in his room and both Millie and Wane's doors were closed. I slipped over to the kitchen and out the side door.

The small window in the door let in some light from the lamp that hung outside above the fountain. I looked out the window and could see the lamplight exposing a soft, drizzling rain. I couldn't see Kate or Milo and wondered if they would

really come. I had a feeling Milo might show, but I was doubt-
ful about Kate. Girls always talked big, but when it came down
to it Kate would probably want her beauty sleep instead. Ten
seconds later I heard a soft scratching at the door.

I pushed the door open and Milo and Kate squeezed in.
Milo was carrying a big stick; Kate had a turned-off flashlight.
I was happy to be wrong about her.

"Sorry we're late," Kate whispered. "Milo walks so slow."

I held my finger to my lips and nodded for them to follow.
We made our way to the far hall and then down toward the
door. The house was so dark and there were hundreds of doors,
but I felt pretty sure I had found the right one.

I tested the knob. Still locked. I pulled the key from my
pocket and slipped it into the lock. Just like the night before, a
crisp click echoed in the hall—of course last night someone else
had turned the key from the other side.

Kate held onto my sleeve as I pushed the door open. We all
stepped inside and I locked the door behind us.

There was a faint light seeping out from under the wall and
through the hole I had created last night. I motioned for Kate
to hand me her flashlight. She did so and I flipped it on. A tight
beam of light shot out like a saber. I sliced the light through the
room to get a better look around and to make sure we were
alone.

The windows were covered with black paint and there were a few broken pieces of furniture scattered around the room: a table that leaned, a chair with a missing arm, and a wardrobe with peeling paint and a warped top. I opened the wardrobe to make sure nobody was inside of it. It was empty. I was surprised to see no other door or opening in the room. Someone had been in here last night and had opened the door for me. It creeped me out to think that whoever it had been had probably been in the room the whole time. I wondered how anyone could have gotten out since I had locked the door from the outside. I checked the window and it slid open easily. The light rain blew in, making the space smell wet. I closed the window.

"This isn't a basement," Kate pointed out.

"I know," I whispered. "It's down there."

I shined the flashlight against the wall, illuminating the small hole my foot had made.

"We go through there?" Milo asked.

It did seem rather impossible. The wall was covered in a thick floral wallpaper and the hole looked more like part of the pattern than the opening to a basement. I flipped off the flashlight and as our eyes adjusted, we could once again see light coming from the hole.

Milo crouched down and looked through. "Wow," he whispered.

"Shhhh," I insisted.

"Move," Kate said, softly dropping down herself.

"Why would someone fill in a basement?" Kate whispered. "It's so weird."

I reached down and stuck my fingers through the hole. With almost no effort at all, I pulled up and the hole tore quietly. I tugged harder and the hole became a two-foot-long tear.

"More," Kate said, getting to her knees.

Both Milo and I pulled at the hole, ripping the wallpaper and busting out a nice long chunk of plaster. The hole was the size of a small person. I could see the dirt tunnel and the edges of some buried stairs.

"Who wants to go—"

Kate wasn't waiting for an invitation; she pushed through the opening as far as she could, but it was still too small. She pulled back out.

"It needs to be a little bigger," she whispered.

We all took hold of different parts of the hole and slowly pulled. The wall broke open like a wet cracker. I tore off bits of hanging wallpaper and dropped them to the floor. As scared as I was, I wasn't about to let Kate go first again. I took a deep breath and flipped on the flashlight again.

I bent down and put my right foot on the top stair. I had to duck my head and squeeze through, but with a little effort I wiggled all the way in. Kate was right behind, pushing me to move further so she and Milo could get in.

"Hold on," I whispered, already regretting my decision to go first; the small tunnel made it difficult to move.

Kate and Milo squeezed through as I slowly made my way down the dirt-covered stairs. The tunnel was about a foot too short for my tall frame. My back ached as I reached the bottom of the stairs and the bend in the tunnel. I stopped and Kate and Milo pushed up behind me.

"What are you doing?" Kate asked.

She answered her own question by looking further down the tunnel. There were three different tunnels.

"Which one?" she said.

I turned off the flashlight and waited for my eyes to spot the glimmering light. It was coming from the left tunnel. I could hear something chattering again.

"Can you hear that?" I whispered.

"I think so," Kate said softly. "What is it?"

"I have no idea. Should we keep going?" I asked.

Their response wasn't instant. I was about to turn back when Kate nudged me gently forward. I kept the flashlight off so that if there was something up ahead we would have some element of surprise. Besides there was enough dull light to see our way.

I could see bits of furniture, material, and corners of walls sticking out of the sides of the dirt tunnel.

"Who dug this tunnel?" Kate asked, as if I should know.

"I have no idea," I replied.

"Someone determined. Maybe your uncle," Milo said.

"Why?" I questioned. "And why did someone fill it up in the first place?"

We turned another corner and followed the dirt tunnel about a hundred feet. We passed two or three offshoots, but kept heading toward the light.

"It's getting brighter," Milo said needlessly.

At the end of the long tunnel, seven dirt-covered stairs led down into a space the size of a small bedroom. Against the far side of the room was a desk sticking halfway out of the dirt wall. A wooden stool was resting in front of it. I could see an empty coatrack leaning against the wall, and the hearth of a fireplace stuffed with dirt.

A single candle was burning on the desk. The brass candle-holder sat on top of a stack of dry parchment paper. The air streaming through the tunnel rustled the papers and sent the sound of whispering through the air.

"Who lit the candle?" Milo asked.

"Seriously, man, how should I know?" I said, bothered.

I bent down to look at the flame. I lifted the candle up and, like an idiot who didn't think things through, I pinched it out. The room was dark.

"Why would you do that?" Kate said in disbelief. "That was—"

A few tiny sparks shot up as the candle crackled back to life. We all stared at the flickering flame.

"Did you know it would do that?" Kate asked.

"I suspected it would," I lied.

The papers on the desk chattered in the light breeze. I grabbed a few and held the candle close to see if I could read what they said. Kate and Milo leaned in around my shoulders. The papers were covered in big flowery writing that looked like a different language.

Beneath the papers was an old book. It was brown with a raised spine and a raised image on the front. There was so much grime on the book that I couldn't make out the image or what the title might be. I opened the book and flipped through the pages. I saw the word "Pillage" on a few of them.

"What is it?" Kate asked.

"Just a book," I said lamely.

"Cool," Milo said, excited. "It might be important. You should take it."

"A book?" I asked. I held onto the book as the slight amount of wind in the tunnel picked up and began to howl at us.

"Let's get out and come back tomorrow," I said.

Nobody argued with me. I flipped the flashlight on and shined it up the stairs. We moved quickly back down the long tunnel. At the last junction we turned right and climbed back up the stairs and into the room.

Once we were all out of the tunnel, I suggested we push the wardrobe in front of the hole—just in case. Both Kate and Milo saw the wisdom of my suggestion. The wardrobe was much lighter than it looked and it covered the hole nicely.

I walked them to the side door and let them out. It was still raining so they ran quickly away. I turned and cut through the dark kitchen.

"What are you doing?" Wane said, stopping both my progress and my heart.

I shoved the book into the back of my pants. Wane flipped on the kitchen light, gazing at me like I was a formula she needed to memorize. She stood only a couple of feet in front of me, centered in the far doorway of the kitchen. She didn't look happy. She was wearing tight white leggings and a tank top. She looked more like a woman than I had remembered.

"You scared me," I admitted.

"You're supposed to be in bed."

"I was hungry so I came down to find something."

"You could have rang," she said suspiciously.

"This late? I didn't want to wake anyone up."

"I'm awake now."

"Sorry."

"So you were getting food in the dark?"

"I like to be surprised."

Wane didn't smile.

"Did you find something?" she asked.

"I'm not hungry anymore," I said lamely. "In fact, I'm feeling pretty tired."

I ran past Wane and didn't stop until I was in my room. I locked my door and breathed deeply.

"'I like to be surprised'?" I muttered, shaking my head at the lame answer I had given Wane.

I sat down on my bed and looked at the book. There were a number of pictures inside of odd creatures and wild plants. Some of the pictures were of ancient and strange-looking dragons. One illustration in the front showed a dragon emerging from a stone. I didn't mind the pictures, but the writing in the book was tight and cramped and hard to read.

I sighed and shoved the book under my mattress. It didn't help me sleep any sounder.

It is the pillage gift to be able to inspire even the weeds in the field to serve a purpose. But the gift only works as long as the growth feels necessary. It is a gift we have horribly abused.

Excerpt from section five of The Grim Knot, *as recorded by Daniel Phillips*

CHAPTER 11

Ask

IT'S NOT TALL ENOUGH," Milo said, defeated.

"It was the tallest one I could find," I complained, looking up at the ladder. It barely reached halfway up the wall.

"Kate," I called.

"Nothing," she called back.

Kate had been kind enough to stand guard on the front side of the conservatory and to let us know if anyone was coming. I had endured another day of school, this one with no calamity or unexplainable incident. Milo and Kate wanted to go back to the basement, but I felt we should wait until later. And since we had a wait on our hands, I figured the best way to kill some time was to find a way into the conservatory. Scott had gone to town, which made our mission that much easier. I knew that what I really should be doing was my homework and going to bed early, but the desire to figure out what was behind the wall was stronger than my need for sleep.

"What if we threw a rope up there?" I suggested. "Like Batman."

"You mean a grappling hook?" Milo clarified. I could almost see the light going off in his head. "Hold on."

Milo took off running toward the direction of his house. I walked around the corner and joined Kate as she stared off into the distance.

"Nobody yet," she said, keeping her eyes peeled. "Where's Milo?"

"I think he ran home to get some rope."

"You know there's probably nothing behind that wall but weeds," Kate said, sounding like the callous Kate I had first fallen in like with.

"Maybe," I shrugged.

"What then?"

"I'll start obsessing about the basement."

"It must be nice to have options." Kate smiled.

"Is Kingsplot always like this?" I asked. "So odd-feeling?"

"I don't know what you're talking about," she said, turning her gaze from the gardens to me.

Her blue eyes pointed out the deficiencies of the gray sky.

"I feel like there's more than just mist in the air."

Kate tilted her head and smiled. "Milo told me about your mom," she said. "I should have been nicer to you on the train."

"Don't worry about it," I said. "And yes, you should have."

"Was she young?"

"I guess," I answered. "She always seemed old. Well, not really old, but weighed down. You know?"

"Kind of."

"Being her son wasn't always easy, but I miss her now. You know, her journal talks about this garden."

"It does?" Kate asked excitedly.

"She grew up here."

"And you never visited?"

"Something happened," I replied. "I don't really understand all of her journal, but something happened. I didn't even know about Kingsplot until my uncle sent me a ticket."

"I wonder if she knew what's in this conservatory."

I shrugged. "Her journal doesn't mention anything." I watched Kate toss her hair over her shoulder. "What about your parents?"

"What about them?"

"Are they alive?"

"Yes," Kate said. "They're kinda hippies. My mom paints pictures of fruit and my dad's a gardener."

"Does he grow fruit?" I asked.

Kate stared at me.

"You know, so your mom can paint them."

Kate halfway smiled.

I turned from Kate and looked up at the tall, cloud-topped black walls of the conservatory. I let my eyes slowly descend, gazing at the wall for any sign of how to get in. At the base of the walls grew a line of short, thick scrub oak.

As my vision rested on the scrub oak, a thought came to me.

"What do you think made that salad fly around?"

"The principal told us it was the wind." Kate laughed.

"Nice to know we're being taken care of by such brilliant minds," I said. "Wind? Wind that only blew toward Wyatt?"

"I don't know," Kate said. "I was there and I still don't understand it."

"And the ivy the day before," I continued, perplexed. "It picked up Wyatt."

"Milo said it was weird."

I thought about the bush that had warped when I looked at it. I turned my eyes toward the scrub oak and said, "Grow."

The scrub oak began to shake and stretch. Kate heard the rustling and looked over.

"What—" Kate started to say, but stopped in shock.

The leaves reached up as it grew quickly against the wall.

The small branches expanded rapidly, looking like woody tooth-paste being rapidly squeezed from a tube. The bushes grew taller and taller, reaching my shoulders in no time. The weight of the bush, however, became too great and it toppled over, falling to the ground.

"Let's lift it," I said urgently.

I got under the branches and pushed the scrub oak up against the wall. It was still growing.

"A little help!" I asked frantically.

Kate stood next to me, both of us trying to keep the heavy growth pushed up against the wall. The branches above us became too heavy and flopped down, pulling us to the ground.

I rolled out of the scrub oak and told the bush to stop. Kate got to her feet and stared at the huge pile of folded over scrub oak. The bush had stopped growing, just like I'd told it to.

"How did you do that?" she asked, dumbfounded.

"I've always been good with plants," I answered, equally stunned.

"My dad's good with plants," Kate whispered in awe. "But he could never do that."

"I told you, there's something in the air."

"So . . . you really did make the salad fly?"

"I don't know," I said. "I think it was just looking out for me."

"You're not normal," Kate said, stepping back. "This is not normal."

I opened my hands and looked at my palms as though there might be an explanation printed there.

"I can't explain it."

"I don't believe it," Kate replied.

We both looked back at the enormous scrub oak.

"You know, if it would stick to the wall, we could climb it."

"The wall's too slick," Kate pointed out.

I instantly thought of the bricked-in archway on the back of the conservatory.

"Come on," I said, reaching for Kate's hand.

Surprisingly, she gave it to me. We ran around the conservatory to the archway. On the ground below the arch was a scrawny patch of purple ivy. I looked at Kate and shrugged.

"Grow," I pleaded.

Just like that, the ivy began to crackle and squeak as it stretched upward. Large purple leaves bloomed and thick, woody strands of vines reached up the wall like greedy fingers looking for something to clutch. The weight of the ivy caused it to lean forward a bit, but tiny feelers reached out and grabbed hold of the textured bricks. Thousands of tiny shoots spun out like cobwebs, grasping the bricks and climbing the wall.

The ivy lunged upward, taking a better hold with each brick

it touched until the wall was covered with a thick, four-foot wide strip of growth. A tight, stretching sound crackled through the air. I stepped back and watched the ivy creep over the stone letters and into the mist.

"Seriously," Kate said, looking at me. "That's not normal."

The noise stopped and the ivy settled. I looked up, grabbed hold of a thick vine, and pulled. It felt as if the ivy was woven into the stone.

"I think it could hold us."

"What about Milo?" Kate asked.

"He'll come eventually," I answered.

"You first," Kate said.

I reached up as high as I could and put my left foot into the ivy. The ivy was wet, but the texture of it made gripping it easy. I pulled myself up. After a few minutes I looked down, surprised at how high I was. Kate was still on the ground.

"Come on," I yelled down.

I pushed up into the mist until I could see the top edge of the wall. The clouds were so thick I couldn't see clearly if Kate was climbing behind me.

I moved quicker, wanting desperately to see what was in the conservatory. My hands reached the top and I pulled myself up onto the lip of the wall. I looked down, but the mist was as thick as soup and I couldn't see anything.

The ivy curled over the top of the wall and ran down the inside. The thought of climbing into the closed area alone was seventy percent intriguing and thirty percent frightening.

I finally saw Kate coming up through the fog. She was breathing hard and climbing fast. I reached down and helped her onto the top of the wall.

"Great," she said, taking deep breaths. "I can't see anything."

I slipped my legs around the ivy and began climbing down into the walled area.

"We don't know what's down there," Kate said.

"That's why I'm going," I replied.

It was even easier to climb down. The thick mist clung to me like wet cotton candy. I grabbed each strand of ivy carefully, making sure my hold was solid. After I climbed down about five feet, the mist started to break up and I could see soil down below. I climbed faster. In my haste, my right foot and left hand slipped simultaneously and I fell the last four feet to the ground.

The soil was soft and splashed up around me like thick water. I rolled to my feet, holding to the dangling ends of the ivy for support.

I looked around in awe. The inside of the conservatory felt huge. Scattered around the grounds were eight small, large-leafed plants that stuck straight up out of the soil in a systematic pattern. In the center of the conservatory stood a small shed with a tiny, windowed door and thatched roof. A narrow brick path cut across the soil to the shed and then led to some wide metal bins on the far side.

It was eerily quiet.

Kate stepped down off the ivy, arriving in a far more dignified manner than I had. She looked around, taking in each detail.

We both looked at the shack.

"Come on," I whispered.

We followed the brick path to the small shed. Kate knocked as though we were neighbors stopping by to borrow some sugar.

Nobody answered.

I tried the knob and the door opened, the hinges groaning in protest. The room was small, maybe eight feet by eight feet, and was thick with dust and at least a hundred cobwebs. The floor was wood except for in the center of the room where a circular pit was covered with a metal grate. Sitting on the metal grate was a burlap sack that looked to be filled with something heavy and lumpy. It was also covered in spiderwebs.

"Cozy," Kate whispered.

"What's in the sack?"

"Look and see," Kate prompted me.

"I hate spiderwebs," I admitted.

"You're not impressing me," she said dryly.

"I'm not trying to impress you," I said, bothered that she would even think that.

"Well, whether you're trying to or not, you're failing."

I hated girls.

I pushed through the cobwebs, blowing the few that stuck to my face out of my way. The burlap sack was covered with actual spiders, but as I reached down, they scurried off, disappearing into the shadows.

I grabbed the bag by the bunched-up neck and tried to heft it. There was no way; it must have weighed at least two hundred pounds.

"If you can't lift it, just open it," Kate said, still standing at the door.

"Thanks," I snapped.

I pulled the top of the sack back and untied a band of material that was twisted around it. The neck of the bag opened about a foot wide. Light from one of the small windows poured over the sack, letting me easily see inside.

The bag was filled with dull-colored stones—some were oval, some were almost square, and I could see a couple that were flat and long. I reached in and pulled one out.

The single rock must have weighed at least thirty pounds.

"They're really heavy," I said.

"I can see that. Bring one out."

I awkwardly carried the stone to the shed's door where we could both look at it in the gray air. Kate wanted to hold it, but the weight of it made her change her mind.

"I've never felt anything so heavy," Kate said, giving it back to me. "What is it?"

I remembered the illustrations I had seen in my book last night. "I think it's an egg stone."

"An egg stone?" Kate laughed. "What in the world is an egg stone?"

"For a dragon," I said seriously.

Kate laughed again. "You're serious?"

"I don't know. That book we found had pictures of them."

"Oh," she mocked, "pictures? That settles it. So these rocks are dragon eggs?"

I wished I had never said anything about dragons.

"I can make plants grow and lettuce fight people," I pointed out. "What's so crazy about dragon eggs?"

"Plants are real."

"Good point," I said, embarrassed. "I'm being stupid."

Kate patted me on the back as if I were some sad, defeated little kid.

"We should probably go," I said. "Scott will be home soon,

and I don't want him dragging me back to the house by my ear again."

I put the stone back in the bag and we walked across the dirt toward the ivy. Kate was saying something about how all guys wanted dragons to be real when she tripped and fell to the ground. I helped her up, happy for the chance to hold her hand.

"You okay?" I asked.

Kate looked at the ground where she had tripped. There was a six-inch hole and something black and metal showing. I got down on my knees and stuck my finger into the hole.

Kate made a hissing noise and I pulled my hand back quickly.

"Seriously," I said. "You're hilarious."

I stood up and kicked at the hole with my shoe. More ground broke loose, falling down a long, straight hole. I could see that the black metal was actually a bar.

"It looks like a cage," I said.

Kate started to kick at the dirt while I jumped up and down. The dirt resisted at first, but then it broke apart like moist cake and slid down into darkness. Kate screamed as a ten-foot section dropped from beneath her feet.

"It *is* a cage," I said excitedly.

She moved back while I continued to push dirt through the bars. In a short while, we had the entire top cleared off. The cage was probably twenty by ten feet and ran lengthwise along the wall with the arch. Uncovered, it looked like a large cattle guard.

"Maybe it was to stop animals from coming in here when the arch was open," I said.

"Or to keep something from getting out."

A loud thump sounded from behind. I jumped about two inches higher than Kate did. Turning around, I saw that a large metal horseshoe had landed in the dirt. A long length of rope was tied to the horseshoe. It began to move, dragging through the dirt as it was pulled up and ultimately back over the wall.

"What's that?" Kate asked.

"I think it's Milo's idea of a grappling hook."

Kate and I climbed out of the conservatory and down the other side. Once we were both back on the ground, I gave the ivy a little instruction and the branches and vines crawled back down the wall until it had returned to its original size.

We walked around the wall to find Milo trying to throw his horseshoe again.

"Where'd you guys go?" he asked.

"Inside," Kate said casually.

"How?" he asked excitedly.

"We'll show you tomorrow."

"That's not fair," Milo whined.

"You guys should get home," I said. "Your parents will be getting concerned."

"My parents aren't concerned," Milo complained. "They're in town, shopping for a new stove because the one we have doesn't work and all the food we eat is cold. Have you ever had cold corn? It tastes . . ."

Milo trailed off as we stared at him.

"Fine," he said defensively. "But I didn't run all the way home to get this rope just so we could give up and . . ."

In the far distance, the sound of Scott's hounds could be heard.

"We'll show you later, I promise," I said. "But for now I've got to go."

"Then what about the basement?" Milo asked. "Let's check out the basement."

"Not tonight," I pleaded. "I don't want Scott to catch me in the gardens. Plus it's late and I'm tired. Tomorrow's Friday; we can stay out later."

Milo argued with me for a bit before accepting my excuses. He frowned, obviously upset.

The hounds were getting louder.

"I'll see you guys on the bus," I waved. I took off running through the forest as Milo and Kate ran in the opposite direction.

Bruno watched the nest grow bigger around the stone. He didn't sleep for days staring at what was happening. In the end, the nest opened, exposing the stone and changing his life forever. The peddler's curse had mistakenly created one very dangerous miracle.

Excerpt from section six of The Grim Knot, *as recorded by Daniel Phillips*

CHAPTER 12

Two-Quarters of a Person

I HAD BARELY FALLEN ASLEEP when a rap on my bedroom door woke me up. I still was not completely comfortable sleeping alone on the third floor. Between the unexplained noises and the mysterious wind and my imagination running wild, sleep was a precious escape that was not always easy to achieve.

Now that I had fallen asleep, someone had the nerve to knock on my door.

"Who is it?" I asked groggily.

"Wane," she replied through the door.

"Door's open," I mumbled.

Wane came in and flipped on the light. She smiled at me. "Nice hair," she joked.

"I wasn't planning on seeing people in the middle of the night," I said defensively.

"Sorry," Wane apologized. "I'd rather be sleeping myself, but your uncle wants to see you and he has no sense of time."

My heart rate increased. I was suddenly wide awake.

"Come with me," Wane said. "And hurry."

I jumped out of bed and threw on my shirt. Wane was already out the door and walking down the hall. I raced to catch up to her.

"Why now?" I asked.

"Who knows?" Wane shrugged. "He found out you were here and demanded to see you."

"He didn't know I was here?" I asked in amazement.

Wane stopped and looked at me. I could see her thinking behind her eyes.

"No," she finally said. "Well, kind of."

"I thought he sent for me?"

"I'm sure he would have if he had been aware of your situation. But your uncle doesn't communicate well with others. Millie acted in your best interest."

We climbed the stairs to the fourth floor, crossed the hall, and moved up to the fifth.

I looked at Wane. She was pretty even at night. "Do you like working here?" I asked, suddenly curious.

Wane stopped climbing the stairs. "Of course."

"It doesn't seem like the kind of question that can be answered with an 'of course.'" I pointed out.

Wane smiled.

"Sorry," I said. "I mean, it seems like a weird job, and unless you lost a bet and *have* to work here, you'd be better off doing something else."

"This is my home," she said simply, beginning to climb again.

After a few steps I spoke again. "I'm glad you're here."

"Thanks, Beck."

We walked across an open, empty room.

"Remember what we've said," Wane insisted. "You are not to worry him. If he asks about the manor, give him only good news. Bad news makes him . . ."

"Makes him?"

"Just stick to the good news."

On the sixth floor was an archway with a large brown door. Wane took a key from her pocket and opened it. I was tempted to inform her that I had a key similar to hers, but I didn't.

Once through the door, Wane put her hand on my shoulder and turned me around to look at her. The room was lit softly by lion-shaped sconces.

"He wants to see you alone," she said.

"Is that bad?"

"You'll be fine," she said unconvincingly. "Through that door is a spiral staircase that will take you to the dome room. Knock before you enter."

"Can't this wait until morning?" I asked anxiously. "Like when it's light? Or when I'm at school?"

"Go," Wane said unsympathetically. "Waiting will only make him more . . ."

Wane stopped herself again.

"More what?" I panicked.

"Hurry," she said, pushing me. "He's waiting."

I was no longer glad Wane was here.

I walked toward the door slowly. I looked back at Wane and she motioned for me to keep going. I went through the door and began to climb the spiral stairs. The staircase twisted for a hundred feet before stopping at a trapdoor in the ceiling.

I wanted to see my uncle—at least I thought I did. My whole life I had longed for my dad to show up and take me away. Now I had an uncle I hadn't even known about and I wanted him to step into the role. I was tired of being alone and ignored. I thought Uncle Aeron could make my life better. At least those had been my thoughts before I had arrived in Kingsplot. Now I felt that maybe my life was fine with just me.

I knocked on the trapdoor and a muffled voice answered.

"Come."

I pushed the heavy door up and open. It fell back against the floor with a loud knock.

"Come, come," my uncle insisted. "Close the door behind you."

I climbed up into the dome room and closed the trapdoor behind me. The room was warm and the floor was covered with thick furs. There were windows open all around the circular room. A small bed rested off to one side and there was a pot near the foot of the bed. Next to one of the windows stood an antique telescope with books and blankets scattered around the base of it.

And sitting on a chair next to a burning candle and looking directly at me was my Uncle Aeron.

He looked a bit like my mother, though with a long beard and wild, gray hair. He had deep brown eyes, and his tattered bathrobe made him look like a homeless actor in a community production of *Lord of the Rings*. In his right hand he held a long black staff covered with markings. I didn't recognize any of them. The inside of the dome was painted with a map of the world.

"You guys must like maps," I said.

"Beck?" Uncle Aeron whispered reverently.

I nodded, not knowing what else to do.

"Come here," he insisted. "Come."

I walked up to him. He held me at arm's length and looked me in the eyes as if searching for something deep within me. He looked like a person who would have given just about anything to smile, but didn't because of pride.

"Francine," he whispered sadly. "Your mother?"

I nodded.

"She would never have let you come."

"What?" I asked, bewildered. "I thought—"

"Where is she?" he interrupted.

I didn't like this at all. I wasn't supposed to give him bad news and what could be worse news than telling him what happened to his sister?

"Where is she?" he asked, agitated.

I had no choice. "She's dead."

My uncle let go of me and stood. He gazed out the window, looking at the stars as clouds moved over and above them as though he could see her spirit in the sky. He kneaded his toes in the furry pelt on the floor.

"You shouldn't have come."

"I kinda had no choice," I pointed out.

"It's far too dangerous here."

"I don't understand."

"You came by train?" he asked frantically.

I nodded.

Aeron began to pick up books, madly flipping through the pages.

"What's the condition of my estate?" he asked.

"I don't know what you mean."

"The manor?"

"It's really nice," I tried.

"I should wander down, but I must watch the skies," he said sadly. "The staff? How are they?"

"You mean Millie, Thomas, and Wane? Oh, and Scott?"

"That's only four."

"That's all there is."

"Ridiculous," Aeron said. "There are hundreds; you'll meet them later. And the gardens?"

"Can't you see them from here?" I asked in confusion.

"Don't be smart," he said, banging his staff. "I must watch the heavens."

"But you looked at me," I pointed out. "And you look at your books."

Aeron turned. I wished he wasn't looking at me at the moment.

"You don't understand," he whispered slowly. "You're a child, faced with an equation you can't possibly figure out."

"That doesn't make sense," I said, hating the way grown-ups insisted on talking.

"You sleep in the manor?" he asked quickly.

"I do," I answered. "On the third floor."

"Good. You play where you should?"

"I think so."

"There are poachers in the woods—stay clear of them."

"Poachers?" I asked, thinking of someone cooking eggs.

"Hunters going after my game. Stay clear of them," he ordered again. "Francine . . . your mother was a strong person. She was wise to leave here."

"Why did she?" I asked.

"It was our plan."

Aeron saw something flutter in the sky. He ran to his telescope and looked up. With his right eye still to the lens, he continued. "She hated so many things about our family. When she left, she vowed never to step foot in Kingsplot again."

"Why?"

"She was trying to run away from what she knew would happen."

"What was going to happen?"

"I don't know yet," he said sadly. "It's only just beginning."

I didn't like the sound of that.

"What's up with this family?" I complained as sincerely as I could. "No one says anything straight."

"Our father, Morgan, was a harsh man."

"See?" I argued.

He wasn't listening to me.

"Not only did he disapprove of whom Francine loved, he had not wanted to wake up our mistake," Aeron explained. "What of your father?"

"I have no idea," I answered, summing up my feelings about our entire conversation. "My dad left my mother when I was just a kid."

Aeron adjusted the telescope. "No Phillips stays married for long."

He was a crystal-clear communicator; no wonder he lived alone.

Silence fell as a soft wind blew through the room. I was pretty confused. I was also worried that if I didn't ask now I might never know the answers to some of the things that were bothering me.

"It seems weird here," I said.

"Eh?"

"Here in Kingsplot. There's lots of things . . . growing," I said awkwardly.

Aeron took his eye from the lens and looked at me with confusion. "What's that supposed to mean?"

"I've seen bushes grow really rapidly and—"

He looked for a moment like he might be proud of me, but

then he swore and grabbed my shoulders. "Stop it!" he said. "Stop it right now."

"What?" I said, shaking loose from his grip.

"It's a curse, a perversion," he insisted, pointing at me with short, skinny fingers. "The land we own trusts you because of who you are. The plants are not looking to do good—they're looking to use you. Not a single Phillips has ever benefited from our control of the foliage."

"I don't understand."

"Have you been to the gardens?" he asked, worried. "The back gardens?"

His tone was so grave that I felt I needed to lie. "No."

"Good," he sighed. "Stay away from the back gardens."

"What about the growing?"

"You're a Phillips." He shrugged. "It's something in you."

"I don't understand what that has to do with me being able to make salad fly."

"It's using you," he muttered darkly.

"Who?" I asked in confusion. "The lettuce?"

"Careful," he warned. "You are treading with heavy feet where the ground is still brittle."

I needed a translator.

"Why don't you come down?" I asked. "Come down from the roof. Walk around the house; tell me about my mother."

"Foolishness." He peered through the telescope again.

I shook my head and decided to take another tack. "Someone said there was a basement here."

"Who said that?" He shoved the telescope away so quickly I heard the metal creak.

"A boy at school," I said, scared.

"School," he hissed in derision. "I suppose Squall is still there."

"He is," I said, surprised.

"Ever since . . . well, he's never cared for our family." He shook his head. "And Wales?"

"What?" I asked, thinking he was asking about whales that lived in the sea.

"Principal Wales," Aeron clarified. "He's still manning the helm of Callowbrow?"

"Yes."

"Humor him," my uncle said. "But place no confidence in what he teaches. Now what boy told you tales of a basement?"

"I don't know his name," I lied.

"You are a poor liar," my uncle said sadly. "And there is no basement."

I wanted to accuse him of being a poor liar as well but I held my tongue.

"Can I visit you again?" I asked. I didn't care that Aeron was half a person living a fraction of a real life, I wanted more than anything to have the connection of family.

Aeron saw something float by in the sky and reached excitedly for his telescope. He looked at me, surprised I was still there.

"Go," he ordered, rapping his staff against the floor.

I opened the trapdoor.

"Beck?"

I turned back to look at him.

"I see Francine in you."

"Is that good or bad?"

"It's the truth. Now go."

He turned his attention back to the skies. I turned my attention to the stairs and made my way back to my room.

Once you have awakened the stones, there is no turning back.

Excerpt from section seven of The Grim Knot, *as recorded by Daniel Phillips*

CHAPTER 13

I Wonder

I THOUGHT ABOUT WHAT MY UNCLE said all night. I even dreamed about him and my mother scolding me for not being responsible and telling the truth about having found the basement. When I woke up in the morning, Wane was sitting on the edge of my bed, wanting to know what my uncle had told me.

I kept it very vague.

After school, Milo, Kate, and I met at the conservatory again and like magic, the ivy slowly climbed the wall at my command. Milo was pretty impressed. He did a weird sort of happy dance as he watched it grow.

"You okay?" I asked.

"That's just so cool."

I shrugged, glancing at Kate, wondering if she thought the same thing.

We all scaled the wall and descended into the conservatory.

"What is this place?" Milo asked.

"I have no idea."

We walked around the entire inside of the conservatory. We got down on our stomachs and peered into the underground cage. The floor was covered with a thick layer of the dirt we had knocked down yesterday. It was a tall cage. If I were to stand inside of it, my five-foot-eleven frame would probably only reach the bottom third of it. We could see a small door with a large lock at the bottom. What we couldn't see was how anyone could get to that door since the tunnel leading to it didn't appear to go very far.

Frustrated by the mysterious cage, we walked around the rest of the conservatory, looking for answers. Beneath the metal bins near the shack, we found a pipe with a rusty handle. When I pulled on it, water flowed out of the pipe and filled the bin.

We walked over and stood by one of the eight plants.

"What do you think they are?" Kate asked.

"I wish I knew."

"Didn't your uncle tell you anything?"

"Not really."

I knelt down by one of the plants and looked closely at it. "It looks new," I said.

Milo wanted to see what was in the shack, so we went inside. We cleared out the webs and dusted things as well as we could. One by one, we brought all eight stones out into the gray light. We laid the stones out on the ground and took a few moments to look at each one.

"Maybe they're just rocks," Milo said.

"Maybe." I shrugged. "And maybe the ivy just happens to grow fast whenever I ask it to."

"I know things are weird," Kate agreed. "But there has to be some explanation for all this."

"Let me know when you think of it," I replied.

"There are eight rocks," Milo said suddenly.

"So?" I said.

"There are eight plants," Milo pointed out.

"Coincidence?" Kate asked.

I picked up a stone that had a yellow line running through it. It was heavier than lead. I pulled it up to my waist and shuffled over to the closest plant. I set the stone down on the soil as though I knew what I was doing. The rock sank a few inches into the dirt.

I looked at the tiny shoot of green next to the rock and

kindly asked it to do whatever it was it was supposed to do. No one was more surprised than I was that the plant listened.

The sprout began to twist up before bending down and burrowing into the earth. The soil sizzled, and in a few seconds a small, green nest blossomed on the ground with the stone tucked neatly inside.

"Wow," Milo laughed.

"So, is that what it's supposed to do?" Kate whispered in awe.

"I guess so," I whispered back.

"Do the rest," Milo said excitedly.

As quickly as we could, we moved the stones into place—setting each stone near each plant. One thought from me, and the tiny green shoot sprang up, lifting each stone out of the dirt and into a cozy nest.

"Can you make them grow higher?" Milo asked.

As much as I concentrated, though, I could not get the nests to expand or the plant to lift the stones any higher.

"What now?" Kate asked.

"I have no idea."

As if on cue, lightning lit the low clouds and thunder ripped through the air. Seven seconds later, heavy raindrops smacked down all around us. We ran to the shed and closed the door.

The rain picked up, deep puddles forming all over the yard.

The ground in the area was already so waterlogged, the puddles filled up quickly. The noise of the rain against the thatched roof was deafening.

"We have to get out!" Kate yelled.

Thunder shook the shed.

"I'm not climbing over that wall with lightning going off!" Milo screamed.

The rain increased in strength, beating against the window violently. Water ran off the shack in torrents. I couldn't see the soil outside anymore.

"The conservatory couldn't actually fill up, could it?" Milo asked, panicked.

"Don't be stupid," I replied. "It would take days to fill this place. The walls are too high."

"I can't swim," Milo announced.

"Would you relax?" I snapped. "We'll be fine."

A bolt of lightning struck the roof of the shack at the same time the clap of thunder knocked us to our knees. My ears rang from the sound and my eyes burned with white light from the flash. I could smell something thick and oily.

"Smoke," I muttered, shaking my head. "I smell smoke."

"The shack is on fire!" Kate yelled at me.

I looked up, wiping tears and rain from my eyes. Huge orange flames were eating holes in the thatched roof. Dark black smoke boiled across the ceiling and flowed down the walls. I coughed hard enough I saw stars.

We couldn't stay here. Already the temperature was rising in the confined space. The fire would destroy the entire shack in just a few minutes. With us inside.

"What are we going to do?" Milo shouted.

Lightning ripped through the conservatory. We couldn't escape across the courtyard.

I fell to my knees, running my hands over the floor, looking for the metal grate where the sack of stones once sat in the center of the shack.

"Here," I said as my fingers latched onto the grate. "We can get out through here." I pulled on the grate and it shifted slightly. "Help me lift this, Milo."

Kate knelt down by me and Milo and all three of us pulled. The grate came loose and we shoved it to the side. I turned to look down the long hole.

"Where do you think it goes?" Milo asked.

"Down," I said, stating the obvious.

"There's no way I'm going in there," Milo said. "What if it just leads to that cage?"

"Then stay here and burn," I snapped. I could feel the heat from the flames licking at my skin.

Thunder rocked the air and another lightning bolt shook the ground.

"I'm going," Kate said, bending down to slip into the hole.

"Let me go first," I insisted. "We don't know what's down there."

She let me push her out of the way and I sat down on the edge of the hole with my legs dangling in the dark. Raindrops were falling through the ruined roof, sizzling with the heat of the fire all around us. My shoes found a small, protruding step in the wall.

"There's a foothold here," I exclaimed.

I lowered myself into the hole. The air was a little cooler here but I knew it wouldn't last long. My right foot found another ledge.

I descended further. I couldn't see anything and smoky air filled my lungs each time I tried to talk. I glanced up to see Kate's legs stepping down right above me.

Three more steps down and I could feel the floor. I jumped down and felt around, trying to get some idea of where I was.

A thin stream of water trickled down the hole and started to pool around my ankles. With the shack gone and the grate open, nothing would stop the rain from flooding the tunnel. I didn't want to escape burning to death only to drown instead.

Kate splashed down next to me in the mud. We moved

down the tunnel, trying to put as much distance between us and the rising water.

"Where's Milo?" I asked.

His feet splashing down answered for me.

"I can't see anything," Kate said needlessly.

"We should go back," Milo pleaded. "I bet the fire's out by now. Maybe we could get out."

"I doubt it," I said. "Come on."

I moved down the tunnel, feeling my way in the dark. Kate had her hand on my belt and she instructed Milo to hold onto her hand. The water around our feet was rising.

"We should go back," Milo kept saying. "We have no idea where this goes. What if it goes nowhere? What if the water keeps getting higher?"

"I guess we'd die," I said, tired of him freaking out.

"We should go back," Milo yelled again.

The water was almost up to my knees and the tunnel was still pitch black.

"Go faster," Kate begged.

"I can't see anything," I said, growing concerned myself.

We had reached a point of no return. The water was rising and we were deep enough into the tunnel that even if we were to turn around, we might not get back to the hole before the water completely flooded the tunnel. We all seemed to realize it at the same time.

"What do we do now?" Kate whispered.

I was crouched over, trying to step as wide as possible, hoping that I didn't walk over an unseen edge or into a wall.

"This was a stupid idea," Milo muttered.

I was going to argue something back, but the tunnel floor suddenly dropped out from beneath me and I fell five feet into a large room filled with water. I flailed wildly under the water, struggling to get up for air. But Kate still had hold of my belt. She fell hard right on top of me, pushing me deeper underwater. We twisted around, trying to untangle ourselves just as Milo—who still had hold of Kate's hand—joined the wet party.

I thought I would never taste air again.

Just before my lungs gave out, I surfaced, gasping in the dark, wet air. I could hear Kate and Milo coughing and choking as they surfaced behind me. I swam a little ways away from the sound of the falling water and my hand brushed up against the lip of another tunnel. I was able to pull myself up and stand. As my eyes adjusted to the darkness, I could see Kate in the water and reached out to help her up. I did the same for Milo. We could hear the water rushing through the tunnel and falling into the pool in a constant waterfall. At least we were safe on dry ground.

"Where are we?" Milo asked.

"Well, I'm pretty sure this will lead us to Buckingham Palace," I said sarcastically. "How would I know where we are? Come on." Once again, I could feel Kate holding onto me.

I began to move forward, but as if to punctuate my point of not knowing where we were, I ran right into a dead end.

"Perfect," I snapped.

"What now?" Kate asked.

"We can't go back," Milo whined. "It's too dark. And I can't swim across that pool."

"We have to go back," I pointed out. "There's no other way."

"Wait," Kate said. "Do you see that?"

"What?" I had no idea what she was looking at. I could barely see my hand in front of my face.

"The wall," she said. "It's glowing."

I felt the dead end and tried to see light.

"There's something there," Milo said excitedly. "I can see cracks of light."

"I can't see anything," I admitted.

Kate moved around me and started kicking at the wall. Nothing happened. Milo tried and still nothing. I thought they'd both gone tunnel crazy, so I had them move back and I kicked the dirt wall with my right foot as hard as I could. My leg broke through the wall of dirt and into another opening. A small wash of light dripped into our space. My leg was stuck in the wall.

"I think you're right," I said, not too proud to admit my mistake. "But I think I'm stuck."

Kate and Milo tore at the tunnel where my leg was. Large chunks of dirt broke free and in less than a minute, my leg was freed. There was a big hole in the wall, so we easily slipped through and into the lighted area.

"I think we're in the basement," I said happily.

Instantly the mood became more hopeful. There was a faint trace of light further down the tunnel we were standing in. We followed it and eventually entered a room where a candle was burning. We were in the basement, but in a different room than we had been in before. There were four beds sticking out of the dirt walls and an empty fireplace on the opposite side.

"Wow," Milo said. "Someone digs amazing tunnels."

"But why?" I questioned.

"We should get out before we're discovered," Kate said nervously.

I picked up the candle with my wet hand and the water doused the flame. But like the other candle we'd discovered in the basement, this one came sparking back to life too.

"Come on," I said, leading the way.

We wandered through the tunnel system for at least a half

an hour before we stumbled across the room we'd been in before. In the course of our wanderings, we had found three more rooms that had been partially dug out. One was a kitchen of sorts; another was a room filled with paintings. The dirt had been cleaned off the paintings, but they were still stuck in the walls. The paintings were of stuffy looking people wearing white wigs. The third room we had found was a library. Only four shelves had been dug free, but we spent some time looking at all the books. Most of them were written in foreign languages. There was a whole shelf about making your own pottery and another section about fire and gardening.

When we finally found the stairs leading out of the tunnels I was more than a little relieved. We pushed the wardrobe out of the way and entered the room with the locked door. I didn't have the key with me, so we climbed out the window. It was still raining tigers and horses. We stuck to the back edge of the manor and hiked around the tall shrubs to the front walk. We gathered under a drenched willow tree to assess what had just happened to us.

"I'm not sure what all of it means," I said. "But now we have two ways into the conservatory."

"Tomorrow, we should check to see what the storm did to the stones," Kate said.

"At least it's the weekend," I said. "I needed a break from Callowbrow. Let's meet here tomorrow."

"What time?" Milo asked.

"Ten?" I suggested.

"I'd better go," Kate said. "My parents are going to be wondering where I am."

"Mine too," Milo said.

I felt jealous of them for having parents. "Yeah, go on," I said. "I want to read that book I found. I'm sure it's full of really good information."

They smiled and then ran out into the rain and toward their homes.

Milo shouted, "Happy reading," as he took off.

I stood under the willow listening to the thunder and hoped Millie had something hot and delicious waiting for me.

She did.

The victims will be tending to their lives and without signal or sound, the pillaging will begin.

Excerpt from section seven of The Grim Knot, *as recorded by Daniel Phillips*

CHAPTER 14

How Long Until Now?

IT RAINED FOR THREE DAYS STRAIGHT. Then the temperature dropped and it began to snow. Although I suppose *snow* is too mild a word—it *dumped*. The statues in the driveway were completely hidden by piles of the white stuff. One morning we couldn't open the door because it was frozen shut. Once we had managed to open it, the snow was six feet high and blocking our way out. Millie had clapped her hands and claimed it had never snowed so hard in Kingsplot before. Thomas argued that it had, insisting she was too old to remember properly.

I wanted desperately to get back to the conservatory to see what the rain and snow had done to the shed and stones, but the weather was too vicious. I tried going through the tunnels, but on my first try I got lost. I found my way on my second try, but the part of the tunnel where the water had flowed in was frozen and I couldn't get through.

The only advantage to the huge snowstorm was that school was cancelled. Of course then I had nothing to do but wander the house and see if my key would open any doors.

Fortunately for me it opened most of them. Unfortunately for me most of the locked doors opened to nothing but empty and abandoned rooms.

Wane had brought me a skateboard, and I wasted a couple of afternoons skating around the house. It was fun, but I wanted Kate to be there so I could show off. It wasn't as satisfying performing for Millie and her one good eye.

I wanted to talk to my uncle again, but my key wouldn't unlock any of the doors that opened to the seventh floor. I tried to pick one of the locks with a screwdriver, but the lock was so solid all I managed to do was scratch up the wood and bend the screwdriver.

I spent a lot of time in the kitchen listening to Thomas and Millie squabble with each other and Wane complain about how the snow was keeping her from her boyfriend, Ben, who lived in Kingsplot.

It was the fourth day of the snowstorm when the flakes finally stopped falling. I helped Thomas clear a path to the garage where he was able to get the snowplow and begin clearing the drive.

"I think it's stopping for good," I said as I came in from shoveling. The only snow clothes I could find in the house were old, outdated things that someone had already worn many times before. They were all way too big for me. I took off my jacket and hat and threw them on the floor.

"It's supposed to warm up a bit tomorrow," Wane added.

"I think it looks beautiful," Millie chimed in as she kneaded a large ball of dough. "We've needed the moisture."

I looked at Millie as if she were crazy. It seemed to me that all grown-ups were programmed to say things that sounded grateful no matter how difficult the situation.

"'Needed the moisture'?" I questioned, hopping up to take a seat on the counter. "I've never seen anyplace so irriguous."

"Irriguous?" Wane raised an eyebrow.

"Sorry," I apologized. "It's that stupid dictionary you got me."

Wane smiled.

"Well, the water won't hurt," Millie insisted.

I liked Millie. She was like the grandmother I never had—or more like the grandmother I might have had, but never met.

A bell chimed through the kitchen. Millie and Wane looked over at the ringing bell with surprise.

"I've already brought him lunch," Millie said quietly.

"Who?" I asked.

"Your uncle," Wane answered. "That's the dome bell."

"Maybe he wants some company," I suggested.

I had never seen Millie really laugh before.

"I'll go," Wane sighed.

"I'm coming," I said, jumping down from the counter.

Wane said nothing to stop me from following. I didn't speak until we were past the third floor.

"He just sits up there all day?"

"Pretty much."

"He never comes down? He never surprises you by showing up in the kitchen and asking for something to drink, or asking if he can make cookies?"

Wane rolled her eyes. "No."

"Why?"

"I grew up here," she started, again demonstrating quite clearly how an adult could never give you a straight answer. "My mother worked for your uncle. She died a number of years ago."

"I'm sorry about that," I said honestly.

Wane stopped climbing the stairs and smiled at me.

"It's no fun, that's for sure, but I guess you know all about that. Ever since I can remember Aeron has stayed up in the dome."

"But why?" I asked, frustrated that I couldn't get a straight answer.

"He's watching," she whispered.

"Watching what?"

"We're not sure," she admitted. "The best we can figure is that he feels something will attack by air and he's the watchman."

"So he's crazy?"

"A lot of weird things have happened in this house."

I was so relieved to hear someone else admit that.

"I don't know how many of those things have to do with your uncle's condition," she added. "Strange things can happen in any house. Millie says he entered the dome the day your mother left."

"Really?"

"Millie and Thomas have managed the manor for him."

"Since my mom left?" I asked in amazement.

Wane nodded.

I couldn't believe it. My uncle probably didn't know what a microwave or the Internet was, much less what to do with an iPhone or a Wii. I had seen his room and wondered how one person could exist in such a small place for so long.

"How does he shower?"

"We bring him hot water and a sponge. Millie takes him meals; Thomas buys him clothes. I read to him on occasion."

"Read to him?"

"There are a few books your uncle likes read to him over and over."

"What about a bathroom?"

"Didn't you see the pot?"

"Ewww," I gagged.

"Yeah," Wane said, sounding equally bothered. "Imagine having to clean it."

"Tell me again why you like to work here?"

Wane smiled. "It's only until I've saved enough money to travel. Come on—he's waiting."

"I don't think I wanna go," I said.

"Come on," Wane waved, taking the steps two at a time.

We crossed the sixth floor and reached the arched doors. Wane pulled out her set of keys and opened the lock.

"Wait here," she ordered.

She climbed the spiral stairs and I could hear her muffled voice saying something. She climbed back down and said, "You're up."

"What?"

"Turns out you were right." She smiled. "He just wanted someone to talk to."

"I'm not changing his pot," I insisted.

"Hopefully he won't ask you to."

I climbed up the spiral stairs and through the trapdoor. I looked at everything with new eyes, realizing that my uncle had seen and used nothing but what was in his room for the last twenty years.

Including the pot.

"Hello," I said, closing the trapdoor.

It was colder than before. The violent snowstorm had left the dome room feeling like a freezer. My uncle stared at me, his brown eyes churning. His hair looked longer and his beard even wirier than when I had last seen him.

"Beck." He threw a fur-lined robe at me.

"Uncle." I pulled it on, grateful for the warmth.

"Call me Aeron," he said sadly.

"Aeron."

There was a nice awkward pause. I cleared my throat. "You wanted to talk to me?"

"No clouds." He pointed.

The sky was remarkably clear.

"They'll be blowing in from behind us," he said.

"Oh," I said, looking out the window. "Mystery solved."

"Sometimes I think the weather is trying to force me to move down into the house," Aeron said absently.

"I guess that wouldn't be the worst thing," I tried. "I mean it's a lot warmer downstairs."

"I've been up here for many years," he said mournfully.

I wanted to tell him about the conversation I'd had with Wane and the information I knew, but I kept quiet.

"I've not been lonely before."

"Oh," I said, not knowing where this conversation was going.

"I miss Francine," he admitted.

"Me too."

I had been around creepy people before. My mother had had a number of boyfriends who had given me the willies, and we had often lived near neighbors who made me uncomfortable enough that I'd walk a block away from their place. Certain people just give off bad vibes. My uncle lived on the top of a mansion, looking at the sky, and using a pot for a bathroom. Arguably he should have been at the top of my creepy list, but there was something familiar and honest about him that made me not worry.

"She was an amazing person," he said.

"She was," I said, remembering the time my mother had locked me out of the apartment for two days because she thought I was somebody else.

"She gave up a lot."

I didn't know if he was saying she had sacrificed a lot, or if he was insinuating that she threw in the towel too often. I felt the second definition was more fitting.

My uncle gripped his staff tightly. I watched his knuckles flash white and color slowly return to them.

"It hasn't snowed like this in years."

"That's what Millie was saying," I said.

He looked at me and banged his weird staff against the floor. He spotted a flock of birds in the sky and watched them closely as they flew by.

"If it weren't for this dome over my head, I could be snatched up," he whispered. "They'd snatch me up and it'd be over."

"Those birds?" I asked, confused.

He looked at me as if *I* were the mentally disturbed one.

"Don't tell the others about my condition," he insisted.

"I won't," I promised, reluctant to point out to anyone just how crazy my uncle was.

"Stay out of the gardens."

I nodded.

"And the basement," he added.

"I thought you said there was no basement."

"There isn't."

"But stay out just in case?" I asked.

Aeron took his staff and stared at the markings that ran up and down the wood.

"How is school?"

"It's been cancelled for the last few days because of the snow."

"Simon will make you do more work than if it hadn't snowed."

"Simon?" I asked, not sure if Aeron was talking about a person or if we were suddenly playing a game of "Simon Says."

"I miss your mother," he said again, dejectedly.

Sadly, so did I, and never quite as much as I did at that moment. I wanted to leave, but Aeron looked unbearably lonely.

"I miss a lot of things," I said. "It sucks to be alone sometimes."

Aeron looked at me kindly.

"I miss my mom, but I think I miss my father even more."

Aeron shifted and sat down. He seemed to be listening so I kept going.

"I mean, I did a lot of things with my mom," I said. "We'd go to movies and restaurants and parks. I knew that if I served my mom peas, she'd eat them four at a time. Or that if I complimented her hair, she would blush. I knew a ton of dumb little things about her, but I don't know anything about my dad. I guess I miss what I should know."

The wind blew through the open room my uncle refused to leave. It was kind of a nice moment between a confused kid and weird hermit.

"You have brown hair," Aeron said, as if noticing me for the first time.

"I do," I replied.

After another silence, Aeron spoke again. "Your mother would be proud of you, Beck."

"I think she was."

Aeron smiled.

I said good-bye and climbed down the stairs where Wane was waiting for me.

"What did he want to talk about?" she asked me.

"Guy stuff," I joked.

"Oh."

"We talked about soccer and how poorly his team was doing this year."

"Really?"

"What do you think we talked about?" I said, bothered by Wane's questions. "He's a bit eccentric."

"I know," Wane said.

"When I heard I had an uncle, I was pretty excited," I admitted. "I never knew my father and the thought of having someone who was related to me look after me was kind of nice—comforting. But I think he might just be a bit beyond crazy."

"Your uncle cares about you," Wane said.

I stared at her, amazed at the logic adults used at times. I remembered something else I missed about my mother: the way we had learned to communicate almost silently with each other.

"Come on," Wane motioned. "Millie's made a cake."

I sighed—I guess a cake would have to do. I was sick of the snow.

The first dragon grew to full size in a matter of weeks. Bruno fed it the weeds that his gift had helped him grow. The dragon never wandered far from the nest where it had been born. Eventually Bruno chopped the nest apart and the dragon flew off across the Irish Sea. Without instruction, the beast raided a small village in Scotland. By the end of the night, everything the town had of value was in Bruno's possession.

Excerpt from section seven of The Grim Knot, *as recorded by Daniel Phillips*

CHAPTER 15

Me with a Thorn in My Side

Y ES, MR. PHILLIPS," MR. SQUALL said dryly. "What is it?"

"I don't understand," I said honestly, wanting to make sense of what I thought he was saying. "The dragon represented what?"

I had learned years ago that despite what so many adults always said, there really was such a thing as a stupid question. I had asked a number of them myself over the course of my life. But, I had also learned that life required asking stupid questions every now and then.

Squall sighed.

It had been more than a week since the last snowfall and, with the temperature rising quickly, the snow was starting to melt. There were more patches of green and brown on the ground than white. We had missed almost a week of school and

Mr. Squall was determined to cram down our throats everything the snowstorm had delayed.

"Who said anything about dragons?" Squall questioned.

I looked at the book in my hands.

"I mean demons," I said, slightly embarrassed that my thoughts were on dragons.

"What's not to understand, Beck?" he asked tiredly. "The character believed that he could be both physical and immortal. He was a demon who aspired for more."

I rolled my eyes for all to see.

"Come down here," Mr. Squall insisted, motioning for me to approach. "Now."

I shrugged and stood. I closed my book and walked to the front of the class.

"I know out West there is a sloppy casualness," he said, waving his hands. "Here, however, rolling your eyes is a form of poor upbringing."

The class laughed lightly.

"Perhaps you would like to stand here and roll your eyes for the class?"

"Not really," I said.

"It's not a request," Squall said.

I rolled my eyes, exaggerating the motion.

"Again," Squall insisted, folding his arms smugly across his chest.

The class was laughing louder. Squall tapped his pointing stick on his desk as if he were conducting the laughter. I rolled my eyes and added a smirk. The class liked that. Mr. Squall held his palms up to try to quiet everyone. Unfortunately, my poor upbringing kicked in—I rolled my eyes, smirked, and bowed.

"Enough," Squall said, realizing he was losing control of the class.

I rolled my eyes in his direction.

Mr. Squall grabbed me by the collar of my oversized sports jacket and spun me around to look into my eyes. He leaned close and whispered into my ear. "Did Aeron send you to humiliate me?" he hissed. "Does he want to ruin my life twice?" Mr. Squall pushed me away. "Sit down." He turned away to write something on the chalkboard.

I went back to my seat, thinking hard about what Mr. Squall had said.

At lunch, Milo and I talked about finally returning to the conservatory. Kate was eating lunch with the popular kids, but I knew she would come along if invited.

Wyatt passed our table with Ellis and Carl in tow. Ellis made a face, but they knew better than to mess with me, especially when the school was serving coleslaw.

"What about Scott?" Milo asked.

"It's Thursday. Millie said he's taking the horse to the vet."

Our conversation was halted by the shadow of Mr. Squall. He stood hovering over me with Principal Wales next to him.

"Now," was all Wales said, jerking his head toward the cafeteria door.

I stood up and asked Milo to take care of my tray for me.

"Your office?" I asked the principal.

"Now."

After I stepped in his office, Wales closed the door. Mr. Squall leaned against the back wall and Principal Wales took his seat behind the desk.

"Professor Squall tells me you have been disrupting his class. I want to know why, Beck." He said my name as if he had taken a class that told him to do so. "What's bothering you?" he asked.

I decided to be honest. "Dragons."

Principal Wales jumped in his seat.

"Don't be tart," Squall said to me. He turned to Principal Wales. "See what I mean?"

I looked back and forth between him and the principal. They were communicating with each other by huffing and puffing.

I laughed. I couldn't help it.

"What?" Principal Wales demanded. "Do you find all of this amusing? There's a responsibility necessary to learning at Callowbrow."

"I'm horrible with responsibility," I admitted. "My mother wouldn't even let me have a pet fish."

"Don't bring your mother into this," Squall said hotly.

"I could pretend it was someone else who wouldn't let me have a fish if you'd like," I said angrily.

"Now, now," Principal Wales said, trying to keep the conversation under control. "No need to get heated up. We just want to know how we can help."

"Then I'm not in trouble?" I asked impatiently, not wanting to be late for my next class and risk being called into the principal's office yet again.

"Well, that depends," Wales said.

"On what?"

"Listen," Principal Wales said. "I think we may have gotten off on the wrong foot the other day. The Phillips name still holds water in Kingsplot, and we aren't looking to punish you. We have the weighty responsibility of watching over you. We just want to make sure you're not getting yourself into trouble."

Principal Wales's big, round face looked even more absurd when he was speaking nonsense.

"He's not ready for my class," Squall protested.

"Not ready for English Lit?" I laughed.

"See," Squall said, sounding like a baby.

"Quiet, Simon," Principal Wales said, holding up his hands. "Listen, Beck, the important thing is that we put away foolish thoughts—take responsibility for our actions. We can't just roll our eyes and start fights and make up silly stories about dragons."

"I didn't make up a story," I pointed out.

"Yes," Principal Wales said, relieved. "See, I'm glad you understand. No stories about dragons. There have been rumors in the past of your family and . . . well, no more stories. Now off to class."

I stood up and left, having no idea how the world operated when the people in control were adults.

When I got home from school, Millie fed me a huge cinnamon roll. It was probably the second or third most delicious thing I had ever eaten. I then put on my snow boots and announced loud enough for everyone to hear that I was going sledding by myself down by the road.

"There's not much snow left," Thomas said.

He was right of course. The weather had warmed up and the snow had melted fast. All the rivers on the mountain were rushing like wet, out-of-control trains.

"I'll find enough to sled down."

Millie looked at Thomas and I could see him remember something.

"Stay where you belong," he said, glancing back at Millie. His instruction sounded rehearsed.

I walked out of the manor and along the side of the drive. Halfway down the path, I turned and trudged through the woods to the meeting spot.

When I got to the willow, nobody was there. I was surprised at how excited I felt. I couldn't wait to get back into the conservatory and see what had happened to the stones.

Milo and Kate were five minutes late.

"Again," Kate said. "Milo's a slow walker. You're sure that gardener's gone?"

"Positive," I said. "Everyone else is in the kitchen."

There was even less snow than I had thought. Of course, there was way more mud than I had anticipated. Milo got stuck twice, and Kate almost lost one of her shoes. By the time we got to the conservatory, all three of us had high-water mud marks up to our knees.

There was a large pile of snow on the ground next to the bricked archway behind the conservatory. I couldn't see the ivy on the ground, but all I had to do was think about it and bright green vines shot upward, grabbing onto the bricks like drowning victims reaching for a rope. The ivy climbed the wall quickly, grateful to be able to stretch.

"Wow," Milo said.

"Ready?" I asked.

They both nodded. Kate went first, followed by Milo, and then me. The ivy was so easy to climb I wondered why there were no ivy ladders or ivy nets in the world. I figured it was just another thing the adults were missing out on.

All three of us sat on the top of the wall in a cloud of mist, pausing to catch our breath.

"Geronimo," I said, swinging out and climbing down the inside ivy. I landed on the snowy ground and watched to make sure Milo and Kate were coming.

Kate spotted the change in the garden before she was even off the ivy and swore in exclamation.

I turned to see what had made her swear. The shack was half burned. The metal bins were filled with melted snow water and a thin crust of ice skimmed across the top. Where the little plants had been, though, there were now eight gigantic, leafy pods. They looked like they were twelve feet in diameter. A couple of the pods shivered as we gazed dumbfounded at the sight. Each pod had a small round hole on top. And, as if the sight of the huge plants wasn't unnerving enough, each pod was floating two or three feet above their green nest. Thick, bushy weeds blanketed the conservatory grounds.

"What happened?" Milo asked.

It seemed pretty clear to me. "The nests grew."

"And learned how to float," Kate added.

I walked over to the closest nest. I reached out to touch it, but changed my mind because it was shivering like a wet dog.

Kate walked over to one and touched it despite the shivering. "It's warm," she whispered.

"Is the stone still inside?" Milo asked, clinging to the ivy, ready to climb away if things went bad.

I stared at Milo, dumbfounded. "I can make things grow, but I don't have X-ray vision."

I stared hard at the nest just to make sure. Milo kept his hands on the ivy.

"Nothing's going to happen," I assured him. "It's perfectly—"

My assurance of safety was cut short by the sound of one nest beginning to howl. The low haunting noise gave me greater goose bumps than the cold wind. Milo was halfway back up the ivy on his way out.

The howling nest trembled and fell down against the ground. The drop shook the ground we were standing on and caused all the other pods to wobble and fall. Kate fell against me, making me lose my balance. Milo was still up on the ivy, clinging for dear life.

Once the nests settled, they began to whistle and howl through the holes on top.

"Maybe we should go," Kate said, concerned.

I wasn't going to argue with her, but I knew that if I climbed out I would eventually have to climb back in to see what had happened.

"Hold on," I said. "We can't just leave. Don't you wanna know what they are?"

"Okay," Kate agreed. "How about if Milo and I leave and you tell us about it later?"

"Really?" I asked, surprised. "I thought you were much braver than that." Personally, I was scared to death, and the last thing I wanted was to be alone in the conservatory. I figured if I bullied Kate into staying, I would be better off.

Kate growled—surprisingly, she still looked pretty.

"They're not going to hurt us," I said.

"How do you know?" Milo yelled down from the ivy.

"They're plants."

"Floating, howling plants," Kate said, trying to sound brave. "Where are the stones?"

"I'm going to guess inside of those things," I said nervously.

I felt like an idiot. I was shaking in fear because of a big plant. There had been times in my past when I had to go out at one o'clock in the morning and find my mother hiding on the street. It was not unusual for her to disappear and hide behind a business or a home somewhere. I always knew that if I reported her behavior I would become a ward of the state or even shipped off to some crazy relative who owned a strange, gigantic manor where plants had personalities.

"This is stupid," I said. "They're just plants."

I walked right up to the nearest nest and knelt down. I leaned over and put my arms around the leaves. The nest was so warm and I could hear a faint purring.

"Stick your hand in the hole," Milo called down.

I ignored him, concentrating on the nest in front of me.

The hole breathed and a trace amount of air escaped. I looked at Kate and decided to pretend I was much braver than I actually was. I carefully stuck my hand into the hole. The nest was hot and moist inside and as I lowered my fingers, I could feel thick, sticky goo.

That was enough for me. I pulled my hand out quickly. There was a thick, orange snot-looking blob hanging from my fingers.

We all collectively, "Eeewed."

I tried to fling the orange stuff off my hand, but it was

un-flingable. Even worse, it was creeping down the rest of my
hand and moving along my arm.

I'm man enough to know when to scream.

"What can I do?" Kate screamed back.

"Pull it off."

Kate looked at the slowly spreading goo.

"No way."

It was not the answer I was expecting. Here I had dreamed
of having a future together with Kate and she wasn't even girl
enough to extract a snotty substance off my arm to save my life
and open the possibility to us even having a future.

While I was lamenting, Kate picked up a stick and poked at
the orange blob—apparently she did care. The orange goop
moved onto the stick. I took the stick and shoved the goo back
into the pod's hole.

"Okay," I said. "Now we'll go."

Before I could even turn around, though, the pod I had just
poked began to crackle and slowly open. The movement and
noise were strangely mesmerizing. The leaves folded back and
wriggled open, exposing a large, gooey center. In the middle of
the goo was one of the stones. It was glowing. As if on cue, all
the other nests began to sizzle and open, distracting me. The
sound was frightening.

"Come on," Milo yelled down. "Let's get out of here."

Kate and I ran to the ivy. Like a gentleman, I let Kate go first and then scrambled up after her.

A loud pop sounded behind me. I lost my grip on the ivy and fell back down to the dirt. I jumped up and looked around, half expecting to see someone standing behind me with a smoking gun.

There was no gun or smoke in sight, but all the nests were spread open and the enlarged stone in the first nest was cracked.

There was another pop, followed by a bang and two more firecracker-like explosions.

"They're all opening," Kate yelled from her spot on the ivy. "Come on!"

I leapt back on the wall, pulling myself up as fast as I could. It sounded like a battlefield behind me as the report of bursting stones filled the air.

Milo had made it to the top of the wall and was already climbing down the outside. I watched Kate push through the cloud of mist and up over the wall as well.

"Wait!" I yelled. "Kate, hold on!"

All I could see was Kate's face through the mist as she peered back over at me. She looked appropriately worried.

"What?" she yelled. "Hurry."

"We can't just leave," I said. "What are they?"

"You're welcome to go back and look," Kate said, scared.

I glanced down, trying to see through the mist. Kate saw my hesitation and panicked.

"You can't go down, Beck," she said. "I was joking, come on."

I started to move away from her.

"Beck, don't!"

I smiled and slipped below the cloud of mist and out of her view. I didn't feel quite so brave without her watching me.

The popping and cracking had stopped, but the sound of something tittering and chirping could be heard. I looked over my shoulder as I climbed down the ivy, but I couldn't make out what was making the noise. It looked like something in each of the nests was squirming.

When my feet hit the ground, I turned to take a good look at what was happening. My mouth dropped open wide enough to house a full-grown chicken. In the center of every nest was a small, wriggling creature. I rubbed my eyes with my hand and took a better look.

"Uh-oh," I whispered.

The small creatures in each nest squeaked and stretched. They were all different colors and slightly different sizes. Most had large, wide-set blue eyes with protruding noses and big mouths. Some were uglier than others; a couple of them were even cute.

I couldn't believe my eyes.

I had grown up watching plenty of movies and TV shows with realistic special effects. I had seen dinosaurs roaming and witches flying, all thanks to the magic of computer animation. Those things had *appeared* real, but I could tell that what I was seeing now was no special effect, it *was* real.

"Amazing," Kate said right behind me, startling me.

"I knew there was no way you could stay away." I smiled nervously.

I could see Milo coming back down the wall. He slowly let go of the ivy, looking fearfully at what was happening.

"What are they?" he asked.

"I think they're dragons," I answered honestly, half-wishing they were only special effects.

I walked up to one of the nests and looked down at the creature.

"Pick it up," Kate whispered.

Apparently I'm influenced by girls whispering things to me. I reached out and lifted the small creature. It was green and folded like an accordion in my hands. It was cute, but I could see misunderstanding and fire in its eyes. I shifted him to Kate's outstretched hands. She cradled it like a baby and whispered something to it.

I felt betrayed.

"It's beautiful," she said.

"I don't believe it." I stared.

"The evidence is pretty convincing." Kate smiled.

Milo wanted to just look at the creature and not touch it yet. Kate handed me the dragon, and I lifted it up to stare in its eyes. As I did so, it scratched my chin with its sharp back claws.

"Ow!" I said, quickly putting it back in the nest.

We all stood back, gazing at the baby dragons stretching and coming to life.

"Unbelievable," I said in awe, rubbing my scratch.

"Are you okay?" Kate asked.

I realized I honestly didn't know how to answer her.

In 1837, Bruno Pillage sailed across the Irish Sea to Ireland. He had mysteriously amassed a fantastic amount of wealth. Bruno met and married a woman named Catharine. Together, they returned to the Isle of Man and built a large manor and farm. They had one daughter and one son. The son's name was Daniel.

Excerpt from section eight of The Grim Knot, *as recorded by Daniel Phillips*

CHAPTER 16

Is It Really So Odd?

I HAVE BEEN TAUGHT A NUMBER of things in my life. I really can't remember a time when I wasn't surrounded by adults bombarding me with things they thought I should know. I remember learning the moon is 238,855 miles away and that "i" comes before "e" except after "c." Both perfectly useful things to know if you're going to spend some time writing on the moon. Now I felt gypped. Not a single person had ever taught me how to handle and raise dragons. In fact, I had met a number of adults who had insisted dragons weren't even real. I wished desperately they could see me now.

The dragons had hatched two weeks earlier and already we were becoming a bit weary of spending time with them. Not that they weren't fascinating and cool, but they were also huge and powerful and frightening. They were like gigantic, scaly crows impatiently strutting around and growing huge teeth, which they used to consume the hearty, thick weeds growing in the conservatory.

Kate had names for all eight of them: Myth, the fat, spiky one with skin so foggy and gray that she didn't look real; Jane was almost pretty with yellow skin, piercing green eyes, and bright white teeth; Mercury, the silver, metallic-looking one; Ishmael, the big, white one I preferred to call Whitey; Carpet, the extra-hairy one; and Saber, who had two large teeth sticking out of his mouth like a saber-toothed tiger. Kate had named the tallest and skinniest one Rydon because she said it sounded like a dragon name. The smallest one we called Pip for obvious reasons. They all had hairy backs and odd, colorful markings.

Rydon was half as tall as the walls of the conservatory. He was covered in gray scales from the neck down, but his head was orange. He had a nice shaped single horn right above his nose and a fine looking tail covered with sharp, jagged pieces of cartilage. He struggled with walking, but when he flapped his wings, you could feel the air move all the way to the corners of the conservatory. Pip was green with a black stripe down her stomach and white, furry ears. She had the most personality and was really the only one who seemed happy to see us when we delivered extra food and attention.

It had not been easy taking care of them. We spent hours

each day trying to avoid Scott and collect extra food from the forest for the dragons. We figured we should probably be feeding them meat, but Kate said the moment we fed them something that could actually bleed she was out.

Ishmael nipped playfully at Milo's hair, knocking him to the ground in the process. Milo didn't find it as enjoyable as Ishmael did. Milo picked himself up and moved over by Kate and me.

"They're getting a little too big," he said needlessly.

"I know."

"What happens when they learn to fly?" Kate wondered aloud.

"I guess the problem will take care of itself at that point," I said.

"We can't just let them fly away," she reasoned. "There has to be someway to manage them."

Each dragon was possessive of his or her space, rarely moving too far from the spot where they had been born except to drink from the metal bins or to tussle with each other.

"Your uncle has to know something about managing them," Milo said. "This is his place."

"My uncle's a little different," I admitted.

"I told you," Milo said.

"Still," Kate said, watching Pip eat a pile of weeds as big as her. "In a few days these things are going to be too big for even this place to hide."

"I don't know what to do," I insisted.

"What about that book you found?" Milo asked.

"The book from the basement? What about it?" I asked, confused.

"There's a tunnel connecting the conservatory to the basement," Milo pointed out. "Maybe that's important."

I shook my head. "The dragons are important."

"Maybe the book is too," Milo said insistently. "You should read the book more carefully."

Rydon turned and, while spinning his tail, clipped my right side, sending me flying into Carpet, the purple dragon with the thick, hairy back and wings. Carpet didn't enjoy having me dumped on him. He bit my shirt and lifted me up. He shook me like a dog shaking a toy and then flipped me into Mercury's nest. Milo had originally wanted to name Mercury, Shiny, but I had argued that that was quite possibly the worst dragon name ever. So we changed it.

Mercury nudged me. I poked him back with a long stick and he screamed at me. I decided it was time to get out of the nest. I hurried back to Kate and Milo.

"I gotta be honest," I said. "I don't think they are going to take orders from us much longer. I should tell Wane; she'd help us."

"No," Milo said. "They'll take them away or kill them."

"No one's going to kill them," I replied, more confidently than I felt. I knew how much adults loved to take apart and study everything in an effort to keep themselves busy.

"This is so strange," Kate said softly as she looked out over the herd.

"I know," I said. "Dragons aren't even real."

Kate smiled at me.

I held my hand out and she put hers in mine. I pulled her over toward the half-burned shack as Milo followed us. We hefted up the metal grate and Kate and Milo dropped down into the hole. Standing on the small footholds in the wall, I reached up to shift the grate back into place before descending to the tunnel floor. I had wised up days ago and now kept a small flashlight in my pocket for safer tunnel travel. There was no water in the hole, but there were still a few parts that were muddy from ice that had frozen and then thawed.

With no flowing water coming in we had discovered that beneath the shack the tunnel ran in two directions. One tunnel led to the manor's basement and the other led to the huge underground cage. We couldn't get inside the cage because of the massively solid lock holding the door shut.

We headed toward the manor's basement and quickly crossed the underground pool. In no time we passed up the bedroom and the library. I was starting to get the hang of navigating the tunnels.

"You really should read that book you took," Milo insisted.

"I'm working on it," I said defensively. "I've been a little busy raising dragons."

"That book could have something we need in it," Kate said.

"Kate's right," Milo joined in.

"I know, I know." I said. "I'll finish in the next couple of days."

We had reached the room with the desk and ever-burning candle. It lit the room with awkward shadows. We walked straight to the tunnel that would lead us to the back of the wardrobe. While exploring the tunnels we had found another way into the manor, but it came out on the far side of the house, close to Scott's room, so we always used our original entrance.

I turned off the flashlight, knowing the wardrobe room would be dark, but light enough to move around. Kate helped me push the wardrobe away and all three of us climbed out into the dimly lit room.

I thought I was experiencing a flash of revelation. It turns out the revelation was just Thomas flipping on the light switch to illuminate Millie and Wane who were standing on either side of him. They all three wore expressions similar to those I had seen by a few other adults and teachers in my life who had been less than pleased with me.

"Beck," Millie scolded sadly. "I can't believe it."

Kate and Milo moved behind me as if I would protect them.

"What are you doing here?" Wane demanded.

"What are *you* doing here?" I countered instinctively.

"Nothing happens in the house without us knowing about it," Millie said.

"So tell us the truth. What are you doing here?" Wane asked again.

"We were dusting." It was all I could come up with on the fly.

"Dusting?" Thomas asked angrily, pointing his cane at me. I had never seen that color in Thomas's cheeks before.

"I told you to stay out of the basement," Wane said.

"Actually, you said there was no basement," I pointed out.

"That should make our insistence even clearer," Millie argued.

I vowed to never, ever talk or reason like an adult.

Thomas stomped his foot and pointed to the door. "To your room," he said. "And you children are to stay clear of the manor. Understood? Especially you."

Thomas pointed at Milo, but Kate nodded as well. They

slipped out as fast as they could, running down the hallway and out through the door. I couldn't believe how quickly they deserted me.

"I'm disappointed," Millie said to my back as I began my journey to my room.

"Sorry," I said, turning to face her. "We didn't hurt anything."

"Children have no idea how high the stakes of life are," Thomas chided harshly. "Go."

I walked faster. Thomas and Wane followed me all the way to my room. Millie walked a few steps behind them. As soon as I was inside, the door was locked behind me.

"Wait," I argued. "You can't lock me in. What if I need to go to the bathroom?"

"Look in the corner," Wane yelled through the door.

I turned and there in the corner was a pot not too terribly different than the one my uncle kept upstairs.

"No way," I said. "You have to let me out."

"Good night, Beck," Thomas said. "This is for your own good."

Words of warped adult wisdom.

"We'll see you in the morning," Millie called sadly. "You need some time to think about what you've done."

I could hear their footsteps retreating. I fell down onto my bed and rubbed my palms against my eyes. I glanced at the pot and realized that my life was going through a seriously weird phase.

At least now it looked like I could finally do a little uninterrupted reading.

For more than twenty years, Bruno pillaged unsuspecting towns—some as far away as a hundred miles—under the cloak of darkness. But his dragons would never strike on the Isle of Man. They would fly over the Irish Sea, pillaging villages far away. In the beginning, when the dragons would die, two stones would appear. But as the years continued and the new dragons perished, the stones were not always there. Some deaths produced one, but most would die and leave nothing. Bruno began to wake the stones only when there was a real pillaging to be had or at tax time. Then, in the summer of 1852, the peddler reappeared.

Excerpt from section eight of The Grim Knot, *as recorded by Daniel Phillips*

CHAPTER 17

Still Sick

IT TOOK ME A FEW MINUTES to clean up the book. I couldn't get to the bathroom sink, so I had to use a lot of spit and one of my older shirts to wash off the cover. Slowly, a raised design emerged on the front of the book. At first I thought it was a large, smashed flower, but as the grime came off, I could see an image of two large dragons knotted together.

My heart leapt.

I worked on the title below the dragons and in time it spelled out *The Grim Knot*. In smaller words beneath the title, I read *The House of Pillage.*

I liked how the book looked. The worn brown leather and raised front made me feel like I held something valuable and important. I opened up the book and discovered that the title page had been ripped out. There was a short dedication on the next page that read "For the sake of equality." The dedication had an illustration of a dragon's nest around it, though I wouldn't have known that's what it was if I hadn't seen the real thing. The book was filled with a number of handwritten entries and appeared to be a record of one family's history. The word *Pillage* was peppered throughout the pages. I looked it up in my dictionary: pillage—the act of looting or plundering, especially in war.

I hadn't noticed right off, but when I flipped open *The Grim Knot* again, I saw a number of names written in ink on the top corner of the inside cover.

I felt a ribbon of cold wrap around my heart as I saw my uncle's name. If this was his book and if the book was about dragons—and both facts certainly appeared to be true—then my crazy old uncle knew more about dragons than he was letting on. I laid on my bed for a long time, thinking of what the best course of action might be.

It was obvious: I had to talk to Aeron immediately.

I closed the book and got up, only then remembering that I was locked in. My key wouldn't turn in my lock and the door was way too solid to kick down. I triple searched the room for some sort of hidden door or tunnel.

There was none.

I opened the window on the side of my room and looked

out. My room was on the third floor and there was no way I could jump all the way down. There was a six-inch ledge right below my window. I looked up and realized that if I could find a way up to the next ledge I would only be two floors away from my uncle. There were some trees and shrubs nearby, but no matter how hard I concentrated I couldn't make them grow upward and rescue me—I felt empty.

I took another glance at how high up I was. I then looked at the book lying on my bed—I had no choice.

I pushed the window up all the way and stepped out onto the ledge. It was cold outside, with barely any wind. I balanced my weight carefully on the ledge. The manor's rough stone facing provided multiple places for me to get a grip.

I stepped sideways along the ledge, moving slowly and looking for any sign of a way to climb higher. I had to go all the way to the back corner before I found a place where I could scale up. The stones joining at the corner made the ascension to the next level easy.

I decided to stick with the corner and climbed up to the next floor like an inexperienced Spiderman.

A light, bitter rain began to fall.

At the top of the sixth floor, a balcony ran along the entire crown of the manor. I climbed past a huge gargoyle and crawled over the balcony rail. I walked around the entire balcony in the rain—not a single window or door was unlocked.

I needed to get just a little bit higher.

I saw a column of small stained-glass windows. The way they were set in the stone created a small ladder. I put my foot on the sill of the lowest window and began to climb.

I pulled myself up onto the widow's walk above the seventh floor where I could see the copper-topped dome where my uncle lived. It was dark inside the dome. I pictured my uncle standing alone with his long staff. It probably wasn't the best idea to surprise him with my unexpected visit.

I knocked on a glass window near the door. "Uncle Aeron."

The cold rain increased.

"Uncle Aeron."

He stuck his head out of an open window and looked at me as if I were a shadowy vision.

"It's me," I said. "Beck."

"Beck? Again?"

"I need to talk to you," I begged.

My uncle retracted his head and a couple of seconds later the glass door swung open. I walked into the dark room as Aeron pulled the door closed.

"What are you doing?" he asked harshly. "I thought I—"

"I need to talk to you."

He looked down at the trapdoor.

"I couldn't come that way," I said, wiping rain out of my eyes. "Thomas locked me in my room."

"What?"

"They locked me up."

"I'm sure they had reason," he said uncomfortably. "Now leave."

"What?"

"You were not invited."

"I need to know something," I said firmly, pretending I wasn't scared to be around him.

"I'm busy," he insisted.

I looked around the shadowy room, wondering what in the world he was busy with. "They locked me up," I argued.

"The manor can be a dangerous place."

"I'm aware of that," I said. "I've been locked up."

"You should be with Francine," he scolded.

"She's gone," I pointed out. "And I have no one else to go to."

Aeron sighed. "I'm not good with children," he said.

There was nothing new in that statement.

"I climbed up the side of the manor to talk to you," I argued.

"I can't be distracted."

I was sick of it. I had been shipped across the country after losing my mother and was now a prisoner in my own house. I could make plants grow, I had a crush on a girl who didn't seem to care, and I was currently the caregiver to eight baby dragons.

"I found your book," I blurted out.

Aeron didn't even turn.

"The Grim Knot."

Now he turned.

"Where did you find that?"

"In the basement."

Aeron knocked his staff violently against the wood floor.

"You were to stay away."

"Well, I didn't, and now I have your book."

"Rubbish," he growled. "Nonsense. I had the basement filled in years ago. All that information is supposed to die with me."

"Well, someone's been digging around," I informed him.

"Rubbish," Aeron answered hotly.

"I'm not making this up for fun," I said. "I have to know about the book."

He didn't answer.

"What about the conservatory?" I asked.

Aeron looked at me with his dark eyes. "That book was best buried. Fortunately, it takes more than a simple glance to understand it."

"I have to know about dragons."

Aeron's hands shook slightly and I could see a dark change in his eyes, black clouds gathering for a deadly storm.

"Dragons?" he whispered dryly.

"Dragons," I said firmly.

Aeron stared at me. He breathed out slowly, letting his shoulders drop. "Dragons," he finally said. "Well, unfortunately, they are a far more complicated thing."

"I've got all night," I insisted, sitting down on a pelt as far from his pot as possible.

"I can't tell you," he said sadly. "You were taken away so you'd never have to know."

"Well, I'm here now and I'm not leaving until you tell me the truth."

The rain continued to fall, splashing against the windows. Aeron said nothing, only continued to peer into the dark.

"I'm not leaving," I reiterated. "I have to know."

Fifteen minutes later, the rain had stopped and my uncle still had not said another word to me.

"What do I do about the dragons?" I finally asked.

"No," Aeron spoke. "I already told you."

The clouds broke and the night sky came alive in a simmering sea of stars.

"Please," I begged. "I need to know what's happening here."

Aeron sighed and, without turning, whispered, "Search the book, Beck. Like so many other things, it has fallen into your lap. There must be a reason for it."

I wanted to complain about all the things that had fallen into my lap for apparently no reason at all, but instead I said, "I feel responsible." I could hardly believe those words were coming out of my own mouth. "For everything that's happening."

"It will all be over soon," he said. "Go."

His words brought such a heavy feeling to the room that I was happy to go out the glass door and begin to scale my way back to my room.

I know it seems foolish to say this, what with everything that was going on, but something felt wrong. I wanted to blame the feeling on the fact that the walls were slippery and dangerous and that at any moment I could fall to my death. Or that my uncle seemed to speak only in riddles. But the feeling was deeper and more depressing than either of those thoughts combined.

Something wasn't right.

I thought about climbing all the way down to the ground floor and running away, but I had nowhere to go. I had to believe that Thomas and Millie would let me out as soon as morning arrived.

I made it to my floor and scooted along the edge until I was back at my window. I climbed in and closed the window behind me. I was planning to read, but after staying up half the night with my unhelpful uncle, my eyelids were so heavy that no matter how I fought against them, they just wouldn't stay open. I left the book beneath my mattress and fell into a deep sleep.

The peddler wanted the stone back. His poorly executed curse was supposed to destroy the family, but in turn it had made them wealthy beyond imagination. The curse had also caused the peddler to be unable to die until the curse had been resolved. He threatened to expose Bruno and ruin the family. If the peddler had to live forever, he did not want to be poor. Bruno Pillage made the peddler a deal—if he was allowed to send the dragons out one more time, he would give the peddler the rest of the stones.

Excerpt from section nine of The Grim Knot, *as recorded by Daniel Phillips*

CHAPTER 18

Disgusting Lie

I COULD HEAR A SHARP KNOCKING. It pounded loudly and sounded like it was coming from inside my head. I forced open my eyes to see Thomas nailing boards to my window. I bolted up in bed.

"Easy now," Thomas said. "I'm almost done."

"What are you doing?" I asked.

Thomas turned. "It seems you spent some time outside your room last night. We just want to make sure it doesn't happen again. We can't have you falling and getting hurt."

"This is crazy," I said. "My uncle will have a fit."

"I suppose if he actually comes down he might," Thomas said.

I couldn't believe this was happening. I felt like the situation called for pleading.

"Please, Thomas," I begged. "I'm sorry. I won't leave my room again. I'll stay out of the basement."

Thomas turned and laughed at me. "This isn't about the basement," he smiled wickedly. "It's about your dragons."

"My dragons?" I said, dumbfounded.

"It's your purpose for being here," he said. "How easy it was to manipulate the mind of a child." He shook his head.

"What?"

"Blame your family," Thomas said harshly. "Had your uncle acted like a true Pillage, none of this would be happening."

"Pillage?" I asked. "Is this a joke?"

"No," Thomas said. "I'm afraid this is most serious."

"I'll get out," I threatened.

"I doubt it, but if you do, Scott is watching the windows," Thomas said. "He was the one who informed us of your little escapade last night. He's outside right now and, for the record, he does not have your best interest in mind."

"I don't believe this," I said, feeling more frightened than when I had first seen the dragons hatch.

"Do you think it's easy to keep up this manor?" Thomas asked. "We've sold every bit of furniture and spent every dollar your family ever had. We've auctioned off every animal and let go of everyone but the four of us. Tax time is coming and we will *not* lose the manor."

"Tax time?"

"Money doesn't grow on trees," Thomas said.

My head felt like it was going to explode. Thomas nailed the last board to the top of the window, closing out the final bit of natural light.

"I don't understand," I said sincerely.

"This wasn't my first option," Thomas said. "I've done everything I could to get Aeron to take some action. But he's turned his back on the gift your family is supposed to be cultivating. We needed you to wake the dragons."

"Why me?"

"You're a Pillage," he said. "Your ancestors changed your name when they came to America. But only a Pillage—only *you*— could wake the stones. That's why I needed to make sure Francine wouldn't be around to stop you from coming."

He said the last line so sinisterly that my throat constricted and I dry heaved.

"Nice," he said, disgusted. "Just perfect."

"You hurt my mother?" I asked in disbelief, trying to breathe normally.

"She was very ill," Thomas said, unlocking the door and stepping into the hallway. "Her life was fat with turmoil."

"But the dragons need me," I reasoned.

"The dragons need nothing now but permission to pillage,"

Thomas said. "It has been too many years since they have come to life. Our coffers will be full again."

"You brought me here for this?" I asked, exasperated.

"I'm afraid so," Thomas said.

"But Millie said—"

"Forget what was said," he insisted. "It was all a lie. Mind yourself, and you might see the light of day again sometime. I do have a place for you. After all, you're a Pillage."

Thomas exited the room, locking the door behind him. I didn't know what to think or how to feel. But I did know I needed to talk to Kate and Milo. I needed help. I had never wanted a phone so desperately in my life.

I remembered seeing a few phone numbers sketched in the back of my mother's journal. I pulled the journal out of my dresser and flipped it open to the back. There were five phone numbers: one was the pharmacy, one was Pizza Hut, one had no name next to it, and the fourth and fifth belonged to my mother's lawyer, Mr. Claire—four was his office and five was his home. I stared hard at the last two numbers, memorizing the digits.

I put the journal back in my dresser and walked to the window. The boards were well secured. I grabbed the top one and set my feet against the wall, using all my weight to pull the board loose.

It didn't budge.

I let go and dropped my feet to the floor. I walked around the room, searching for a way out, even though I knew perfectly well I was trapped. I tried the door. I tugged at the boards on the window again. I pulled my dresser from the wall, hoping there might be a secret exit behind it.

There was nothing but wall.

I moved my bed, but like the dresser, it wasn't hiding anything surprising. I climbed onto the dresser and unlatched a metal vent on the ceiling. I was more than willing to climb through it, but the opening was at least a foot too small for me to fit through.

"Ahhhh!" I screamed in frustration.

I pushed the dresser and my bed back against the wall. As the bed shifted, *The Grim Knot* slipped out from between the mattresses.

I was grateful Thomas hadn't found it and taken it away. I picked up the book and sat down on the chair in the corner. I switched on the lamp that sat on the small end table and opened the book.

"There was a time when every Pillage had his eyes to the soil instead of the sky . . ."

The first line was much more interesting than I had anticipated. I looked at the little book, flipping it over in my hands.

It reminded me of a small door. The thought of it being my only way out of the room struck me like a lightning bolt. I read on, stopping only when Thomas brought me a bland lunch. By that point I was on my second read and already devising a plan to set things right.

I couldn't believe how I had been fooled, and by whom.

When the peddler returned to take the remaining stones, Bruno Fillage was gone. He had kindly scorched all his land and burned his home to the ground. The peddler cursed the Fillage family again, promising horrid deaths for every male bearing the Fillage name and insanity for the women.

Excerpt from section nine of The Grim Knot, *as recorded by Daniel Phillips*

CHAPTER 19

Barbarism Begins

I HAD ONLY HEARD THE WORD *genealogy* twice in my life—maybe a few more if you count movies. Who knows what half the people are saying in movies? I had to look the word up in my dictionary.

The Grim Knot was full of genealogy, beginning with my great-great-great-very ancient-super old-grandfather, Hermitage Pillage. Apparently he was poor but happy and could really grow things. His son, Edward Pillage, was born in 1790 and he was cruel and really messed up the family.

I could see through the small cracks in the boards that the sun was finally down. I still was locked in the room, but I felt smarter for having read a little in my book.

Thomas brought me dinner. He stood inside the room

watching me eat as if I might have been able to use the dry bread
and mushy potatoes to make a break for it.

After I finished my meal, he let me use the bathroom and
wash up. While in the bathroom I searched for a way out, but
there were no windows and none of the drains were large
enough for me to slip through.

I came out of the bathroom no freer than I had been before
I went in. Thomas was in the hall, blocking the way. I knew if I
were to pile drive him I could probably take him out and get
away. But, despite all the bad things I had done in my life, I just
didn't have it in me to knock over an old man.

Not yet at least.

As I crossed the hall, I tried to reason with him.

"Maybe I can help," I suggested. "How do you know I don't
want exactly what you do?"

"We can't take that chance," Thomas insisted. "In time there
may be a spot for you."

I walked into my room and Thomas locked the door behind
me. I had never really been a prisoner before. It felt awful, but it
also gave me a sense of purpose.

My goal was clear—get out.

I liked having a goal to focus my mental energy. It was hard
to think about my mother dying, or dragons, or worrying over
unknown noises, when I was so centered on getting free.

I spent a few minutes trying to pull up any of the floor-boards. I finally got one loose, but I could see the surface beneath it was too hard to work through. I went through my backpack, looking for anything I could use, and found a screw-driver at the bottom of the pack. I walked to the door and shoved the flathead screwdriver into the lock as far as possible. I twisted it in the metal dragon's mouth but nothing broke loose inside.

Frustrated, I leaned against the door with my eyes closed, cursing. After using a few words that my mother wouldn't have been proud of, I opened my eyes and noticed the large, brass hinges on the door. I grabbed the top one, wiggling to see how solid it was.

It didn't wiggle at all.

The top of the hinge pin was a small, metal gargoyle head and on the bottom of the hinge pin were tiny claws. All three hinges on the door were identical. I jammed the screwdriver into the hinge, trying to pop it open.

Nothing.

I held the screwdriver by the flat end and beat the hinge with the handle. Not only did it not do anything, but the noise was so loud I was certain Thomas would come up to investigate.

I waited a few minutes, listening for his footsteps in the hallway. Silence. I slipped the screwdriver's tip against the door with the length of metal resting at the bottom of the hinge pin, right behind the tiny claws. With the leverage that gave me, I pulled the angled screwdriver toward me.

A satisfying snap rang through the room as the tiny claws went flying into the far wall.

I took the screwdriver and placed the tip under the bottom of the broken pin. With a little effort, I was able to push the pin up and out. The top hinge was open. The middle hinge was more stubborn, and the bottom one was the easiest of all. I slid all three broken rods back in place and sat on my bed, waiting for the house to be quiet and still. I needed to wait at least until Thomas and Wane and Millie were sleeping.

I picked up *The Grim Knot* and read some more. When I finally set the book down, I had no idea what time it was. It felt like I had been waiting and reading for days. I couldn't wait any longer, so I pulled the pins out and tried to pull the door out of the jamb.

Apparently back when the manor was built, they made doors out of lead. It was so heavy that I was afraid it was going to fall in and topple me. I stuck the screwdriver into the jamb next to the middle hinge and wedged that side of the door out.

The door hesitantly slid off its hinges and made a soft but solid *thunk* as it came to rest on the floor. I worked my fingers around the hinge side and pulled inward. The door snapped out of the lock and started to lean toward me. I braced my arms, but it was too heavy. The door came tumbling down. I fell to the ground at the foot of my bed. The top of the door caught the edge of the bed, preventing me from being smashed.

I crawled out from under the door and looked into the dark hall. The hall was empty. I was honestly surprised to not see Thomas and Wane standing there looking disappointed.

I threw the screwdriver into my backpack as well as most of my other personal items. I pulled *The Grim Knot* out from under my mattress and flung my backpack over my shoulder. I was not planning on coming back. Leaving my suitcase and most of my clothes behind, I took off down the hall.

I had been so nervous about getting out of my room that I had not noticed how windy it was inside the manor. The hall was flowing like a stream with thick currents of wind. I made my way down to the first floor and snuck into the kitchen.

The clock on the wall said 12:29. I had been more patient than I'd thought. I grabbed the phone and dialed Mr. Claude's home number. It rang seven times before a very tired-sounding voice came on the line.

"Hello."

"Mr. Claude," I said.

"Who is this?" he asked groggily.

"It's Beck. Beck Phillips."

There was a long pause. "Beck, do you know what time it is?"

I resisted the urge to be sarcastic. "I'm in trouble," I said. "They've locked me up."

"What?" he said, flustered. "You must be mistaken."

I couldn't resist this time. "Right," I said. "They're probably just playing a really competitive game of hide-and-seek."

"I don't know what to say," Mr. Claude admitted, his voice waking up. "They sent for you."

"Sent for me?" I whispered. "Didn't you find them?"

"Well, no. We were searching for any relative of yours and they called. It seemed fateful," he said.

"You don't understand," I argued, fighting to keep my voice down. "I'm in trouble."

"I'm sure it's nothing like that," Mr. Claude said. "They probably just have a different way of raising children than your mother did."

I don't know how adults live with themselves.

"This isn't about raising children," I said. "They are—"

My conversation was cut short thanks to Thomas pressing the cradle on the phone. He was wearing old-fashioned pajamas and looked unhappy about losing any sleep.

I threw the receiver at him and darted out of the kitchen.

The door leading outside was unlocked and I burst through, stepping down onto the drive. Thomas was right behind me.

"Scott!" Thomas yelled.

I ran toward the front of the manor. I threaded through the statues and leapt onto the front lawn.

Someone fired a shotgun into the air.

My heart considered giving out, but I knew that if I fell down now they would catch me. I headed into the trees lining the side of the lawn and ran through the forest.

A second gunshot fired, sounding muffled and far away. I didn't let that slow me, however. I ran through the forest until I couldn't breathe. I stopped to catch my breath before running again.

Six breathing stops later, I was at the edge of a wide river and too tired to go on. I crawled underneath the thick branches of a pine tree and listened for the dogs.

There were a number of things wrong with my life, as well as a long list of things I didn't enjoy about Kingsplot, but at the moment what I most missed was sleep. I used to spend entire days sleeping while my mom was in one of her moods. Now, I hardly got in a few hours a night.

I couldn't hear the dogs. It was cold, but the extra clothes I had put on and the sweat I had worked up running were keeping me warm for the moment. I wanted to find Kate's or Milo's

home, but I had no idea which direction to head. Mr. Claude
had been useless, and I had nowhere to go.

I leaned against the base of the trunk and tried to sleep, but
I couldn't.

When it grew light enough to see, I crawled out of my hiding spot. The woods were alive with animals scurrying up trees
and running across clearings. I saw four elk drinking from the
river only a couple hundred feet away from me.

I looked east where the sun was rising and then began to
walk. After about a half an hour, I recognized how the mountains sloped into the valley and knew which direction the manor
was. I skirted the side of the hill until I could see the far wall of
the conservatory. I stopped and turned around slowly, watching
the area for any signs of life.

It was hard to believe there were dragons in the conservatory. It was so quiet. The mist above the walls held the sound in
nicely.

I hiked behind the conservatory to the bricked-in archway.
There was no ivy climbing the walls. We had been using the
shack entrance lately and I had not left ivy on the walls for fear
of being caught.

I looked at the ivy beneath the archway and it reluctantly
began to grow. I thought about it even harder, but it still moved
slowly.

Halfway up the wall it stopped.

"Come on," I whispered. "Grow."

The ivy seemed bothered by me. It wouldn't move at first, but eventually it pushed up into the mist. I was so focused on the ivy that I hadn't noticed the spot of red sneaking across the garden and coming closer. At first I thought it might be a deer or another animal, but as soon as I could focus on it, I could tell it was Kate. Milo was trailing behind her.

I didn't know how to feel.

I found a spot where I knew they would pass by. As they stepped close, I called their names and waved them over.

Kate hugged me and kissed me on the cheek. It was almost worth being locked up for a reception like that.

Kate and Milo carried small bundles of bound weeds with rocks anchored to them. They were on their way to feed the dragons.

"We've been throwing things over the wall every few hours," Kate said. "It's almost impossible to heave them that high. It takes forever."

"We're exhausted," Milo added needlessly.

"Thomas and Millie and Wane know about the dragons," I said. "They brought me here specifically to grow them."

Milo looked confused.

"Why'd they not let you in the back gardens then?" Kate asked.

"Apparently they heard I was more likely to do something if I was told not to."

"You must be so proud," Kate said. "You've created a nice reputation."

"So what now?" Milo asked.

We sat under the bows of a huge tree and I took a few minutes to fill them in.

Bruno Pillage successfully escaped to America. He changed the family name to Phillips and built a beautiful manor hidden high in the mountains above the Hagen Valley. There were only ten stones left.

His wife was heartbroken over having to leave her home on the Isle of Man. Her mind became soft and she was eventually hospitalized. A short while later, Bruno died. Two years later, his son, Daniel, married a woman named Diana. They had one son named Taft.

Excerpt from section ten of The Grim Knot, *as recorded by Taft Phillips*

CHAPTER 20

Oscillate Madly

I TOLD KATE AND MILO ABOUT what the book had taught me. I told them about my heritage and about Edward and about Bruno losing everything and being cursed by the peddler. I also brought them up to speed about what I learned about the dragons and the stones.

"So your family raises dragons?" Kate asked.

"They don't so much raise dragons as use them to get money when needed," I said. "And Pillage is my real last name. Bruno changed it to Phillips when he came to America. He never used the stones in America. By then he had so much money it wasn't necessary."

"So these are the first dragons in America?" Kate asked.

"I think so. I think Bruno's son, Daniel, woke one of the stones and maybe my grandfather Morgan did too—that's probably why there were only eight stones to begin with. The book isn't exactly clear, but what I think happened was that when Morgan was about thirty, he started desiring the power and wealth the dragons could give him. He told his son, Aeron, what he planned to do, and Aeron begged him not to do it. After Morgan died, Aeron went mad. He bricked in the conservatory so the dragon stones could never be used again."

Kate and Milo stared at me.

"Aeron was worried the dragons would ruin Kingsplot one day," I said. "I think that was when my mother left. I'm not sure because the book doesn't go that far."

"Your family's horrible," Kate said.

"About every other generation," I agreed. "Aeron is fighting to stop it. And my great-grandfather Taft was so committed to stopping the madness that he locked himself up in the cage below the conservatory."

"Taft was in that cage?" Milo asked, disgusted.

"I guess so."

"Seriously," Kate said. "Your family's really horrible."

"Aeron's willing to die to stop this," I argued.

"So what do we do now?" Kate asked.

"We've got to keep the dragons from pillaging Kingsplot."

"How do you know that's what they'll do?" Kate said.

"It's what they do," I said. "It's the only thing they do.

Thomas and Millie need the money to pay the taxes on this estate so they tricked me into waking the stones."

"How do we stop the dragons?" Milo questioned.

"They won't fly until I chop their nests to pieces. But first, there's another thing I have to do before they can fly."

"You're kidding," Milo said, almost nervously. "The book said that?"

I looked at him queerly. "I didn't see it at first, but there was small, hidden writing around the inside cover. It says some pretty interesting things in the fine print."

"So they won't fly without you doing this additional thing?" Kate asked. "Then we're okay, right? I mean, if they can't fly, they can't pillage."

"Not exactly," I said. "If they are not allowed to fly, the dragons will turn on those who own them. They'll destroy everything here, including anyone who tries to stop them."

"So we're doomed," Kate said.

"There is a way to stop them," I said. "There's something hidden in the shack."

I stepped out from under the long, heavy bows of the tree and walked back up to the arched side of the conservatory. Kate and Milo were right behind me.

"Don't look at or talk to the beasts," I said. "According to the book, they will become annoyed and could eat you just for fun. We've sort of been treating them all wrong."

"Are you sure we should go in?" Milo asked.

"Stick with me."

I climbed the ivy and went up over the wall. Reading *The Grim Knot* had given me a weird sense of confidence. My family had controlled the dragons for hundreds of years and ruined many lives. Now, it was up to me to make things right.

As I moved down the wall and below the mist I was so surprised to see how monstrous the dragons had become that I almost lost my grip on the ivy. All the dragons were resting on the ground, each near their nest. All of them except for Carpet and Jane; their spots were vacant and the plants they had once nested in were withered and brown.

I dropped to the ground and looked out over the remaining six dragons. I could hear Kate and Milo land behind me.

"There's only six," Kate pointed out needlessly. "Where's Jane? And Carpet?"

"Dead," I said.

"What?" Milo asked, almost angrily.

"There was some small writing on one of the last pages," I said excitely. "It talked about how the dragons could become weak—even die—if not allowed to pillage."

"How could that be?" Kate asked.

"Their whole existence is one of greed," I explained. "They don't know anything else and their legacy is built on nothing but destroying things."

Mercury screeched.

"They don't look weak to me," Kate said.

"The strongest survive the longest," I answered. "And according to the book, when they die, they disintegrate and just blow away."

"That will happen to Pip?" Kate asked.

"Don't," I snapped. "Don't call them by their name. They already know us too well, and yes, it will happen to her."

Pip was no longer the smallest dragon—she was monstrous.

"I hope she remembers we were kind to her," Kate said.

I walked around the dragons, heading toward the burnt shack. None of the dragons looked up from eating their weeds. I was acting on faith, believing what the book had said about them not harming me if I acted correctly.

We entered the shack and huddled close together. All three of us breathed a sigh of relief, pretending like the burned-out husk of a shack would actually be enough to save us if the dragons really wanted to harm us.

"It should be in here somewhere," I said. "The book said it's hidden in this shack."

"What is it?" Milo asked. "What's hidden?"

"You'll see."

The shack was beyond repair. The fire had destroyed the roof and scorched the walls. There was no place left to hide anything.

I knelt down and ran my hand back behind the beams that held the wall up. The corner beam was rotting at the top and splitting down the middle. I put my hand on the cracked wood and pulled. A nice, long, wedge of wood came loose. It looked like a fat-ended wand. I gazed at it with a smile on my face. It was perfect.

"I don't believe it," I said.

"That's it?" Milo asked.

I nodded.

"What is it?" Kate questioned. "A wand or something?"

"I think so," I answered. "The book said all I have to do is wave it around and say the right words and the dragons will be gone for good."

Kate glanced at Milo nervously. I stepped to one of the large holes in the wall where a window had once been. I looked out at the dragons. I lifted the wand and opened my mouth.

"Stop," Milo said.

"What?" I asked.

"If you get rid of them, won't you lose the manor?"

"I suppose," I answered, lifting the wand higher. "But I can't let them destroy the town."

"Why not?" Milo asked.

I looked at Milo and thought of *The Grim Knot*. True I had woken the stones, but it was my heritage that had caused all this. If my great-great-great-great-grandfather Edward had simply served that magic-selling peddler some food, none of this would be happening. The pattern of my life did seem to point me in the direction of walking away and letting someone else deal with all this. But there was something changing in me. I could see things clearer now and I wanted to be on the right side of things so that when the dust settled I could live with myself. I didn't care if Kingsplot and Callowbrow had been cruel. I couldn't count on things being perfect, but I was determined to do what I thought was right, regardless.

"It's what's right," I answered.

"You've changed," Milo said.

I'm not sure he meant it as a compliment, but I took it as one. I closed my eyes and lifted the wand. I opened my mouth, ready to speak.

"Stop," Kate insisted.

I swiveled, opening my eyes and glaring at her.

"Why?" I asked.

"Come on. Put it down, Beck," she ordered.

I stared at her with narrowed eyes.

"Please," she insisted.

"I knew it," I said angrily. "You're with them."

"What?"

"Do you think I don't know?" I argued. "Pretty convenient of you, coming back on the train the same time I was. Or how about how enthusiastic you always were to go into dragon's lairs or strange tunnels—or making me plant those rocks. I love to think it was my charming personality that made you want to come with us, but I know that's not the deal."

"What?" Kate said defensively. "You're crazy."

"Now you want me to let the dragons live so they can pillage the entire town. That was your plan all along, wasn't it?"

"My plan?" Kate looked hurt. "Go ahead," she said. "Make them all disappear. I don't care."

"Nice try."

"Seriously," Kate said. "I don't care."

I lifted the wand. Kate stood there with her arms folded and her lips tight.

"They'll all be gone," I said. "Forever."

"Good," she snipped.

I opened my mouth as if to say the magic words and, like a frog's tongue, Milo's hand shot out and snatched the wand from my fist.

I stared at him.

"Sorry, Beck, but I can't let you do that," he said.

"What?" I asked, confused.

Milo smiled. "You were a little bit off, giving Kate credit for all the work I did."

"You? But . . ."

"But what?" He smiled. "Milo would never do anything like that?"

As he talked, his personality began exposing itself like a shirt coming untucked. Weird bits of him began to rise to the surface of his being. He was slowly becoming someone else.

Kate stepped closer to me. I wanted to apologize for thinking she was devious and evil, but the moment felt wrong.

"You were the one who said there was a basement," I said reflectively to Milo.

"I needed you to read that book. I even unlocked the door for you. Of course I wanted you to read it much sooner."

"You showed me where the conservatory was."

"Part of the plan," he said, his nose becoming large and bulbous.

"What's happening to you?" Kate said, disgusted.

Milo was no longer a funny-looking kid; he was now a long-haired, gray-skinned, troll-looking creature. Even his clothes were different. He wore a dark green robe and a leather pouch was slung across his right shoulder, crossing his chest and knotted under his left arm. He sighed as if he had just undone pants four sizes too small.

"Those stones belonged to me," he cackled. He was so repulsive it was hard to look at him. "I should never have let Bruno keep that cursed stone."

"You're the peddler?"

The old, ugly version of Milo looked proud. "You're smarter than I gave you credit for. Edward Pillage betrayed me hundreds of years ago, serving me a stone for sustenance. I cursed him, but I never thought my curse would bring him wealth as well. His son, Bruno, made things even worse. They've all died horrible deaths and all their wives have gone crazy, but they got rich. I've simply come to get my share. I am a great magician. The world will see that now. I searched the world over trying to find where your family was hiding. I'd still be searching if not for luck."

"What about your parents and your home here?" I asked.

"I have no parents," he said. "I've been living in a hole by the river since I arrived here."

I wondered how he still managed to always have cleaner clothes than I did.

"This is ridiculous," Kate said. "I'm leaving."

"No, you're not," the peddler insisted, pulling a long knife from his pouch.

"The eggs are gone," Kate reasoned. "It's over."

"Yes, it's unfortunate you woke them all," he complained. "Still the spoils the dragons will bring back before they die will be great. And it is not out of the question that they could leave behind another stone."

"Let Kate go," I said. "It's me you need."

Milo smiled; I hadn't remembered him having so few teeth.

"Sorry, Beck," he said, "but I want to be rich. I'll keep both this wand and Kate close at hand."

"It's not a magic wand," I admitted with a wide grin. "It's just a piece of wood. I knew there was no way Kate—I mean *you*—would let me destroy the dragons if you were who I thought you were."

"Nice work, Nancy Drew," Kate said, shaking her head.

"Plus, you don't know how to manage the dragons," I said to the peddler.

"Once the dragons are flying it won't matter," he said.

"You're willing to destroy Kingsplot?" I asked.

"Kingsplot is only the beginning."

"I don't get it," I said angrily. "Why me?"

"I had to have you," Milo said. "The stones are nothing until your family's gift of growth helps wake them. Aeron was impossible to persuade. He's useless. And since the gift is only passed from father to son . . ."

"What?" I asked, confused.

"Your *uncle* hasn't told you?" Milo smiled. "How nice. Well, Francine wasn't really your mother, she was your aunt. So Aeron isn't your uncle, he's your . . ."

"Father," Kate finished for him.

I turned to look at Kate. I didn't know how to feel. I wanted to throw up and celebrate at the same time. Unfortunately before I could choose which one to do, I heard Milo shout a string of words in another language. The words seemed to hit the back of my head with the force of a thrown brick. My vision blurred, then blackened.

Then there was nothing but darkness.

Taft Phillips married a woman by the name of Esmeralda. They had one son named Morgan.

Taft was a confused and tender soul who couldn't handle living in a mansion that had been funded by pillaging and built on the pain and hurt of so many innocent people. He withdrew from society and from his family. His wife grew to hate him and left him, moving halfway across the world and leaving him with their son.

Angry at her betrayal and afraid

he might use the stones to seek
revenge, Taft locked himself under
the conservatory and sent Morgan—
along with the only key to the
conservatory—to his estranged wife,
who was living in Europe. By the
time she received the key, though,
it was too late. Taft was long dead.
Esmeralda died shortly after
Morgan's arrival, the guilt she felt
at her husband's death driving her
insane.

Excerpt from section eleven of The Grim Knot, *as recorded by Aeron Phillips*

CHAPTER 21

Panic

W AKE UP, BECK. Wake up."
My ears were working, but my eyes were not
yet willing to let in any light.

"Wake up."

I could feel someone slapping me softly on the cheeks. I recognized Aeron's voice, but I still couldn't convince my eyes to open. I wondered how I had gotten into the dome room on top of the manor. The last thing I remembered was talking to Kate and a creepy old version of Milo in the conservatory.

"You must wake up," Aeron said.

I pushed my eyelids open.

Aeron looked relieved. I glanced around, realizing that I wasn't in the dome room like I had imagined. I was still in the conservatory. And Aeron was with me. I couldn't believe it—he had left his room to help me.

I was sitting against a wall inside the shack with a loose rope tied around me. All of the dragons were gone, and the mist had evaporated, giving me a clear view of the sky and mountaintops through the missing roof.

"You're not my uncle," I said hoarsely.

"I know, son," Aeron said softly.

The sensation of having someone call me *son* in a non-sarcastic way was so weird. It felt as if I finally had found a warm bed or socks that fit properly. I closed my eyes and repeated the word to myself. I opened my eyes back up.

"Why?" I asked. "Why did you leave me?"

"It had to be," Aeron said. "Your mother died giving birth to you. Her greatest fear was that you would become like your ancestors. We had to break the chain. My sister, Francine, wanted to help. I couldn't leave the manor because I needed to make sure the problem died with me. It's a sickness within us. I didn't trust myself to get rid of the stones, so I stayed at the top of the manor, never going near them or the conservatory."

"And Francine?"

"Francine was in love with Simon Squall, but she knew you had to leave Kingsplot. When Francine told Simon our story, he thought she had gone crazy and wanted no part of it or her. We

have all made sacrifices to right what our family has done. You
were never supposed to return."

"I'm sorry," I said weakly.

"I'm sorry, too," Aeron said. "But not that you have
returned."

I was more happy than angry. My life had always seemed so
uncomfortable. I had been so focused on the hardship and confusion that I had rarely taken the time to think about good
things ever happening to me. I was overcome with the emotion
of wanting a father and amazed by the possibility of actually
having found mine all at once.

"Are you okay?" Aeron asked.

"I think I'm better than that, but where are the dragons?" I
asked, trying to think straight.

"Milo sent them out."

"How?" I asked.

"He took your shape to fool the dragons. It's a dangerous
spot to be in. You have cared for the dragons personally and
they know you by sight now. He chopped the nests and the
dragons, believing it was you, flew away."

"But it's daytime. People will see where they're coming
from."

"Milo's so blinded by revenge and greed that he can't think
clearly. He's not so different than I was, watching the sky when

I should have leveled my gaze. When the dragons flew past the dome, I could see the large white one looking at me and recognizing the Pillage features. That's when I knew I needed to do something."

"We have to stop them," I said needlessly.

"This will do it." Aeron held up his black staff with the strange markings.

"A stick will stop them?"

"It will if it's shoved through their throat," he said, sounding like a physics teacher simply dealing out facts. "When this staff pierces their throat, it steals their breath. My father, Morgan, created it, but he was too slow to use it before the dragon he woke killed him. It should kill all of them now—all but the last one."

"Why?"

"The last dragon instinctively excretes a sweat that dries its throat hard as rock."

"So how do we kill it?" I asked.

"The dragon will die after it has feasted on . . ."

"Feasted on what?"

"One of us," Aeron said sadly. "It's the curse. No Pillage can actually enjoy the spoils of what the dragons bring. Our greed is ultimately for naught. It was the fate of your ancestors Daniel and Morgan. They couldn't resist waking at least one stone within their lifetime. They had to know what it was like and lusted for the experience. When they did wake a stone, the dragon grew, consumed them, and died. Before the last one from this batch dies, it will have to consume one of us or else it will never rest in peace."

"The book didn't say that," I said.

"*The Grim Knot* isn't a complete history," Aeron said. "The dragons kill the men and the women go insane."

"Nice family," Kate said, crawling out of the hole.

I was so startled and happy to see her that I might have accidentally giggled even though the moment was so heavy.

"You were down there?" I asked.

"After Milo knocked you out, he tied you up," Kate said. "When he wasn't looking, I pulled open the grate and jumped down the hole. He never came after me. I've been waiting down there trying to get the courage to see if it was safe."

"Do you know where Milo went?" Aeron interrupted Kate.

Before Kate could answer, a screeching noise ripped through the air. I looked up, covering my ears. Through the torn roof, I could see a dark silhouette of a dragon flying through the clouds.

The sight was magnificent.

The three of us left the shack, drawn by the sight of the flying dragon.

"Should we run?" I asked Aeron nervously.

I was certain he was about to say something, but Rydon descending into the conservatory captured our attention. His mouth was filled with a crushed pink bicycle, and in his talons there was a blue mailbox and part of a telephone pole.

We were all thinking it; I was simply the first to say it. "That's the treasure they bring back?"

"Seriously," Kate added, "that's just junk."

"I guess times have changed," Aeron said, equally confused. "Not many people deal in gold bricks and silver these days. In the old days, even wood was valuable."

Rydon dropped everything he had and flapped his wings triumphantly. He clawed at the ground as if anxious to fly again.

"Shouldn't you stop him?" I yelled. "Use the staff!"

"Not yet, I need him," Aeron hollered back. "We've got to get to Kingsplot and stop the other dragons before they do even more damage. I've been waiting for this day for twenty years. I'm glad you're here with me."

The next few moments felt like I was watching a movie really close up. Aeron ran from the side of the shack and circled back around behind Rydon. He moved closer, avoiding the dragon's tail, and leapt onto his back, pulling himself up by grabbing at the hair on the back of Rydon's neck.

I thought Rydon would shake him off, but the dragon

looked almost proud. His wide, orange mouth opened and he roared, spitting fire above the conservatory walls.

"I've never seen any of them do that," Kate said, frightened.

Rydon sprang up and flew out of the conservatory, heading in the direction of Hagen Valley. I could see Aeron's form on the back of the beast. Rydon passed a returning dragon in the air— Ishmael. He hovered over the conservatory and then lowered himself, slowly flapping his massive wings. Dirt blew up into my eyes and nose.

Ishmael had a door in his mouth and railroad tracks in his talons. He set his spoils down and danced around proudly. He screamed and blew fire high into the air.

"Stay here," I yelled to Kate, trying to be heard above Ishmael's roar. "I'm going to help Aeron."

"What should I do?" Kate asked.

Ishmael was rocking back and forth. I could see his knees bend and his wings flex. It was now or never. I left Kate's question hanging and ran up behind Ishmael. I tried to jump onto his back like Aeron had done, but I wasn't quite as graceful as my father had been. Still, I managed to get on and wrap my arms around Ishmael's neck. I could feel his wings flapping on either side of me. My hands pushed into his scales as if he were made of clay.

Ishmael blew fire and burst up into the sky. It was hard to

hold on. I wanted to wave at Kate, but I was too scared of falling. The dragon twisted up like a corkscrew and then leveled out. I tangled my hands into the hair on his back as tightly as possible, scared for my life. My feet kept slipping off his white, scaly skin, and each beat of his wings tossed me up and down against his furry spine.

I opened my eyes in an effort to personally witness my own death. We were high in the air. Ishmael swooped down the mountainside and into the open valley. I could see the other dragons in the distance. It looked as if they were picking up bits of Kingsplot and moving them around. The large lakes surrounding the town were covered with mist as Pip and Saber tore apart the center of the city near the town hall and Callowbrow.

Ishmael arched up and then down, shooting through the shorter tunnel that led into town. Two cars swerved out of the way and crashed into the wall. Ishmael burst out of the tunnel and plummeted swiftly down into town like an elevator that had been cut loose. I started to slide forward on his neck toward his head. I dug my heels into his side, looping my legs over the joint where his wings attached to his body. He turned his head just enough to stare at me with his wide right eye. He looked incredibly happy. I would have felt happy too if it had not been for the ground rising so quickly. I could see people running in the street and Mercury flying above me.

Ishmael was gunning for the city's clock tower. He slammed into it, ripping the top of it off with his talons. I could feel the extra weight pulling us down. The dragon flexed his wings, extending their reach, and pumped them to lift us.

It suddenly occurred to me that I had no idea what I was doing. I beat on Ishmael's back with my feet. He spun, bothered by my kicking. I could see Callowbrow. Sections of the roof had been ripped up and I could see Pip tearing apart the trophy case, scooping out lacrosse and badminton trophies with her mouth.

Ishmael skimmed the surface of the town, darting between parked cars and the people who were valiantly running for their lives. Ishmael opened his jaws and picked up a public drinking fountain from the ground. The motion was so jarring I lost my grip and flew from his back onto a wet grassy field.

I tumbled for a hundred feet and ended up on my back, staring up into the sky. I could see stars and rainbows. Then I saw Ishmael fly right over me and away.

A dragon screamed in the air right above me. I looked up just in time to see Aeron shove his staff into Rydon's neck while they were flying. The dragon screeched like a spastic whistle and slammed down against the ground, sliding to a stop a couple streets over.

I ran toward them as fast as I could. People were ducking for cover and weeping. I watched a family run from their destroyed home into another home. I saw Saber swoop down and pull off the entire roof of the home that family had run into.

Rounding the corner, I saw Aeron lying on the ground. Rydon had thrown him a long distance. I knelt down by Aeron and his eyes fluttered open. I thought he was going to say something compassionate and comforting. I should have known better.

"Did you see that thing die?" he asked solemnly.

I nodded.

Aeron got up quickly, and ran to where Rydon's lifeless body was slowly disappearing like a sandcastle being blown away. Aeron walked right up and yanked the staff from the dragon's vanishing neck.

All around us the sounds of chaos and panic filled the air. I watched Ishmael pick up a man and then drop him into the lake, screaming. I could see Mercury trying to lift up a purple car with a female passenger inside.

"We need to go," I said urgently as Rydon continued to disappear.

"We have to wait to see if there's a stone," Aeron yelled. "We have to be sure this ends here."

"I thought there were no more stones!"

"We have to be sure."

"You wait then," I said, grabbing the staff from him.

I ran around a demolished fountain and up behind Mercury. There was an empty car next to the one he was trying to lift. I jumped up onto the car's roof and spun around, attempting to thrust the engraved staff into Mercury's neck.

I missed.

The staff slid off the side of his neck, only scratching him. He looked at me and steam escaped his flared nostrils.

"Uh-oh," I muttered.

Mercury dropped the purple car and shot up into the air, whistling like a shooting star. The woman in the car next to me looked up at me like I was a superhero. I smiled at her and jumped down, trying to be smooth. I landed wrong and went sliding on my face. I glanced back at her. She appeared less impressed than before.

In the distance, Saber, the skinny orange dragon with long front teeth, was marching down the cobblestone main street. With his front legs he ripped up storefront awnings, looking for treasure to steal.

Aeron ran toward me. "Give me the staff," he yelled.

I thought he was going to go after Saber, but as he turned the corner, I could see Pip running wildly after him. I threw the staff to Aeron. He caught it and spun but it was the wrong position to attack Pip. I saw the dragon open her jaws and lower her head to bite Aeron.

"No, Pip," I screamed.

I jumped back onto the car and sprang up, reaching for Pip's back. With one hand I held tightly to her long green hair and with my other fist I beat down on her neck.

It worked—Pip stopped chasing Aeron and shook her head and neck, trying to toss me off. She rocketed up with me barely hanging onto the hair on the back of her neck.

Pip arched her short back and shot like a bullet toward Callowbrow. She dropped through the large hole that had been torn in the cafeteria's roof. It had not been too many weeks ago that lettuce had been flying around this very same room. Pip skidded across the tiled floor and slammed into the wall.

The jolt sent me flying off of her back and into the teacher's lounge. Pip regained her balance and began tearing apart a bank of lockers. She tore a section of seven lockers away from the wall and then picked up a cafeteria table in her mouth. Two seconds later she was gone out of the hole in the roof.

"Are you okay?" a voice asked.

I looked over to see Professor Squall hiding behind a couch.

"I think so," I said, out of breath. "What are you doing here?"

"I was grading tests when the ceiling started to crumble."

"Did I pass?" I joked.

"Your uncle was right," he said apologetically, ignoring another one of my jokes. "I thought they were crazy."

"They?"

"Aeron and Francine," he answered absently. "I was in love with Francine. She left me to take you away. I thought it was just Aeron trying to ruin our lives."

"I know she was my aunt," I said.

"I wasn't sure if you did."

"You need to read her journal," I said. "She mentions you. Of course I didn't know you were the Simon she was talking about. I think I have a picture of you two."

In the distance a dragon screamed.

I stood up and tried to catch my breath. Callowbrow was in shambles. There were holes all over the roof, and a large area of walls had been ripped out. I could see down the hall and there were no longer any front doors.

Professor Squall and I ran along a corridor by the band room, hopping over trash and wreckage. We were steps away from the missing doors and freedom when Mercury dropped down, blocking our way. He looked down the hall directly at us. I could see his large blue eyes smile mysteriously as he recognized me.

"Oh, great."

We inched backward as Mercury folded his metallic-looking wings and ducked his head into the hallway.

"Sorry about that whole trying-to-kill-you thing," I yelled.

He took two steps closer to us and blew a huge fountain of flame in our direction. The fire didn't reach us, but the heat was intense enough to singe my eyebrows. Parts of the hallway caught on fire and lit up.

I was hoping the burning corridor would deter him, but he pushed right through the fire, still looking at me as if he had a score to settle.

"Over there!" Squall yelled. "In the bathroom. We can trap him."

I ran into the teacher's small bathroom with Mercury following me. I climbed up onto one of the sinks and tried desperately to open the single window the bathroom had.

Mercury's head crashed through the door and into the bathroom. His presence made me try harder and I popped the window open and pushed it out.

Mercury struggled to get through the bathroom door and into the small space. He pulled his body in the room, his tail slithering in behind him.

Squall closed the door, making it impossible for Mercury to back up.

I jumped through the window's opening and easily got the

top half of my body out. Mercury blew fire and I could feel it roasting my legs. I pulled my body out of the window and fell into a thick tangle of ivy. Mercury stuck his head and long neck out of the window, trying to grab hold of me. I scrambled from the ivy, smoldering and scratched.

The dragon screamed. He tried to pull his head back through the window, but the size didn't allow him enough space to back out or move. He was trapped.

Furious, Mercury began to torch the ivy and the trees outside the window. It wasn't easy to do, seeing how all of Kingsplot was waterlogged.

I ran back around the corner just as Aeron was shoving his staff into Saber's neck while the dragon tried to pick up a car with his mouth. A group of three citizens with baseball bats watched in awe as Saber's remains drifted off into the wind.

"Aeron!" I yelled. "Aeron!"

Aeron turned and saw me. He actually smiled and picked up the staff that had fallen to the ground. There was so much going on that I barely had time to notice Myth swooping down, aiming for Aeron.

"Aeron!"

He didn't hear me, but managed to jump onto Myth's back as she twisted in mid-air, skyrocketing upward. In the commotion of getting on, Aeron dropped the black staff. I watched it fall to the ground then ran to retrieve it.

The sound of ambulances and gunshots filled the air. I watched as Myth settled onto a large weather vane on top of a beautiful little church. She wrapped her talons around the north and south arrows and pulled up, flapping her humongous blue wings. Two men on the street fired shotguns at her. The buckshot was absorbed by Myth's body. Some buckshot blew holes in her wings, but the holes quickly closed back up.

Myth pulled the top of the church up and shot sideways, clamping down on a streetlight with her teeth before flying up into the air and back to the manor. The sight was frightening but so impressive I couldn't help but stare. I hoped Aeron was still on her back. I hoped even more that he'd make it back to the manor in one piece.

"Beck!" a frightened voice called. "Down here, Beck!"

I looked over to see Wyatt cowering beneath a bench at the bus stop. He was flat against the ground and more frightened than when he had been picked on by the lettuce. I ran over to him and reached my hand out.

"No way," Wyatt said. "What are they?"

"Dragons," I answered.

"Dragons?"

"Come on," I insisted. "It's not safe out here."

Wyatt scooted out, watching the sky at all times.

"I was walking home when that big white one started chasing me," he whimpered. "It got distracted by something and I crawled under the bench. I saw some guy kill an orange one."

"That was Aeron," I answered as we darted across the open street.

"Your uncle?"

"My dad."

We jumped through the smashed window of a bakery, looking for shelter. Everything was a wreck, but it smelled so good. I slipped behind the counter and slid to the floor, out of breath. Wyatt slid down next to me.

"How many are there?" he asked.

"I think there's four left."

"Where'd they come from?"

I wanted to lie. I wanted more than anything to say, "I have no idea." But this wasn't like letting a bunch of bees loose into a ventilation system—a whole town was being torn apart.

"I grew them," I said apologetically.

"On purpose?" Wyatt asked.

"I didn't know what they were."

"You really don't live a normal life, do you?" he asked, almost kindly.

I smiled.

"So what's that?" Wyatt asked, nodding toward the black staff.

"This kills them."

Wyatt looked impressed. "Shouldn't we be out there then? You know, killing them."

"They know we're after them now," I said. "It won't be as easy. We need to attract the remaining ones to us."

"Attract them?" Wyatt said, concerned.

"If they come to us, it will be much easier."

I raised my head above the counter and looked out the demolished front window. I could see the hat shop across the street and a large paint store.

"What are you looking at?" Wyatt asked.

"I remember something I read," I answered. "About how dragons are drawn to gold and silver."

"So?"

"Come on," I said, jumping up.

I reached the window and watched Ishmael latch onto and carry off a hot dog vending cart. We ran out the window, across the street, and over to the paint store. It looked to be the only business that wasn't smashed open. I swung the staff and busted the front window. We carefully kicked shards of glass out of the way and stepped inside. The store was so organized and clean I felt bad about having to come in to take something. I promised myself I would come back and pay for it later.

"What are we looking for?" Wyatt asked.

"Gold paint. Maybe silver."

We found six gallons of gold paint and two gallons of silver. I grabbed a few paint rollers and brushes and a dozen cans of glitter spray paint. We also took four portable lights that could be used to paint at night.

We tossed everything into a shopping cart and hurried across the street and down the back alleyway toward Callowbrow. The cart was heavy and, thanks to everything being torn apart, we had a difficult time finding a clear path. The town of Kingsplot was in total chaos and panic filled the streets.

I could see Mercury's head still sticking out the bathroom window. He was angrier than ever and blowing fire.

"Into the courtyard," I pointed.

A few trees had fallen down in the brick courtyard at Callowbrow. We shoved the small trees out of the center of the courtyard and kicked away the debris. I grabbed a gallon of gold paint and tried to get the lid off. I had forgotten to take a paint can opener.

"What do we do?" Wyatt worried.

I shrugged and threw the paint can down against the bricks. It popped open and paint shot out.

"Start rolling!" I ordered.

Wyatt took a paint roller with a long handle and began to roll the thick, gold paint all over the bricks. I threw another can of gold paint down and then another and another. I grabbed my own roller and joined Wyatt while shooting spray paint with my other hand.

The thick paint quickly covered most of the large open brick courtyard. I could hear a dragon screaming from the direction of the town's center.

"Hurry!" I yelled.

Wyatt rolled paint spastically. "I can't believe we're doing this!"

"Any other time it would be fun." I smiled.

Wyatt looked at me and laughed, rolling paint all over the bricks.

"I'm sorry about all that stuff I did," he apologized while painting. "You know, how I acted."

"Don't worry," I said. "I'm not always easy to get along with."

Pip flew directly over Callowbrow, heading in the direction of the manor. I could hear people screaming and alarms and car horns going off.

I kept painting.

"I think they're dropping off what they've pillaged," I said loudly. "It doesn't take them long. They'll all be on their way back any moment."

I threw the rest of the cans onto the bricks and we spread the silver paint around with the gold. We covered the entire courtyard and then positioned the four, battery-powered lights around the edge of the paint.

"Is this going to work?" Wyatt said, concerned.

"I don't think so," I replied. "But it's all I could think of."

I heard Mercury pitching a fit at still being jammed in the bathroom.

"Wait here."

I ran out of the courtyard and down the corridor. I stepped through a huge hole in the wall and back outside. I pressed my back up against the wall. I could see Mercury blowing fire. I moved along the wall until I was under his neck that stuck out the window. I looked up at his silver scales and realized what a magnificent creature he was. His scales were iridescent and as smooth as ancient river rocks. Thin stripes of red ran down his neck like thread. I would have given anything to keep him—and all the other dragons—as pets, but I knew that as long as they lived, other people's lives would be in jeopardy. I couldn't let what I had started ruin any more lives.

"Sorry," I said, thrusting the black staff through the bottom of Mercury's neck.

Fire fizzled from his mouth and he relaxed, small particles of him beginning to break free and blow away into the wind. I stood up and peered through the window. There was no stone. In fact, there was nothing but an empty bathroom.

"Sorry, Mercury," I said, surprised by the horrible feeling I had in my chest. My heart felt swollen and raw. Seeing the dragons disappear was more depressing than I had anticipated. I had always wished that dragons were real, and now that I had helped bring some to life, I was getting rid of them. I knew I had to, but it felt dark and confusing.

By the time I got back to the courtyard, Wyatt was hiding behind a short wall and I could see the first of the dragons coming back from the manor.

"Only three left," I said sadly.

"That's a good thing, right?" Wyatt asked.

"Yeah," I answered. "I can see now why my ancestors had such a hard time getting rid of them. They've kinda grown on me."

"Not me," Wyatt said.

A terrifying screech ripped through the air.

"Hit the lights!" I yelled.

The portable lights were directed upward into the air. I was hoping the light would act as a magical dragon trap, but in the daylight, the glow barely registered. The courtyard of gold-painted bricks just looked like a courtyard of gold-painted bricks.

Our lack of lighting didn't stop the dragons from being interested though. Pip was the first to arrive. Drawn to the gold bricks, she dropped into the courtyard with her talons wide open. The thick, wet paint came as a surprise to her, causing her to slip and fall almost directly in front of me. I didn't waste a moment. I tried to shove the staff into her neck, but missed and fell onto my face. My teeth knocked together with a thick click. Pip looked at me, then wrapped her right talon around one of the lights, lifting it into the air and taking it with her as she flew away.

Wyatt looked on open-mouthed.

"I missed," I said lamely.

"I noticed that." Wyatt smiled uneasily.

Myth entered the air space above the courtyard. She began to claw at the worthless bricks like a tractor with blades. The moment Aeron had informed me that we would have to pierce the neck of every dragon, I instantly thought of how difficult it would be to kill Myth. She had the shortest neck of all the dragons and a spiny collar covered the little bit that showed. I knew it would take precision and a whole lot of luck. To make matters worse, I think she had seen me try to kill Pip.

Myth lifted her head, looking at me, confused.

"Hey," I complained. "It's not personal."

Myth replied by blowing fire at me, singeing the front of my shirt. I dropped to the ground and rolled around to her back side. I climbed to my feet, but I couldn't reach as high as her neck. So I threw the staff like a javelin.

I missed and the staff pierced Myth's right shoulder.

In fairness to me, my mother—or rather my aunt who had raised me—had never let me join any sports teams. I was not half-bad at basketball, but throwing things straight was a talent I hadn't yet perfected.

Myth was confused and angry by what I had done. She lowered her head to take a bite out of me, but I was able to twist away, grab hold of the staff, and swing onto her spiky back. She bucked wildly, sending me flying through the air. The black staff flew into the corner of the courtyard.

By the time I was on my feet, Wyatt had already grabbed the staff and, standing on a wall, he jammed it in the exact right spot on Myth's neck.

Myth looked at me and closed her eyes. Her four legs curled into themselves and she shriveled into a pile of dragon bits that scattered around the courtyard. There was no stone.

"Wow," Wyatt said, out of breath. "She was distracted by looking at you so I took a chance."

"Thanks," I said, wiping sweat off my forehead. "Only two more."

We waited in the courtyard, listening to other parts of the town being ripped apart by Ishmael and Pip.

Clouds were moving in, blocking the lowering sun from beating down on the torn-up pile of gold-painted bricks.

"Wait here," I said to Wyatt.

"What?"

"I'm going to see where they are."

"I'm coming with you," he insisted. "There's nothing I can do if they show up."

The streets were filled with tipped-over cars and small chunks of roof and wood. Ishmael was ripping the metal siding from the water tower. Once enough bolts were pulled free, the tower burst and water fell like a flood from above, rushing through the archway of the railway station.

Ishmael stood beneath the waterfall as it cascaded down on him. He was at least five hundred feet away from me. I couldn't believe how huge he was. He looked bigger than the entire conservatory.

I glanced at the staff in my hand and wondered how something so little could stop something so huge. There was no way I could do it alone.

"Are you game for taking down another?" I asked, holding the staff out to Wyatt.

"What do you mean?"

"I'll get him to come near me and then you put him out."

"That's crazy," Wyatt insisted.

"I know."

Wyatt reluctantly grabbed the staff and I took off running toward Ishmael. He was tearing apart the waterlogged railway station, looking for something of value to take. His large claws tore the roof off in long, wide swaths.

Two policemen were in the street, pointlessly firing pistols at him. Ishmael found the railway station's safe and picked it up with his mouth.

"Ishmael!" I screamed.

He didn't hear me. I picked up a good-sized rock and threw it at his knee. I wasn't too sure if he would even feel it, seeing as how the police were still shooting at him, but I took a chance.

"Hey, Whitey!"

He turned and looked down at me. He cocked his head, his mouth full of safe. He took two steps in my direction. The ground shook and the windows of a nearby red car shattered.

I turned and ran as Ishmael began to chase me. It was not easy to run through the mess. Kingsplot looked like a town that had been chewed up and then spit out. Which, I reflected, wasn't that far from the truth.

I jumped over fallen telephone poles and large holes. I couldn't see Wyatt, but I had no choice but to put my faith in him. I stumbled and fell to my knees. Gravity spun me and I ended up on my back, looking skyward as Ishmael approached. He appeared even more massive than before.

The sky darkened with clouds and a light rain began to fall. I held my arm up as if it would help protect me from Ishmael. He landed, standing directly over me. He spit the safe out and it crashed against the road in a shower of sparks. He raised his head and blew fire straight up like a fountain.

Ishmael swung his large, white head toward me. He flared his nostrils and I could feel the pull of air as he breathed in. His mouth was a few feet away from me. He pulled back his lips, showing me all of his teeth. Hot saliva dripped on my forehead.

"Wyatt!" I hissed out of the side of my mouth, not even knowing if he was still around.

Ishmael opened his mouth and his long, thin tongue lolloped out. He retracted it slowly, running it over his lips.

"You can't eat me," I reasoned. "I planted you."

Ishmael opened his mouth even wider and a second row of teeth emerged behind his front row. His head dropped in closer, and his mouth began to close around me. I could feel tips of his teeth pushing against the sides of my head.

I suppose, all things considered, there are much less impressive ways to die.

The danger ~~~~~~~~~ most don't
~~~~~~~~~~~~~~~~ beware of the
tug. ~~~~~~~~~~~~~~~~~~~~~~~~ one
~~~~~~~~~~~~~~~~~~~~~~~~ even you
~~~~~~~~~~~~~~~~~~~~~~~~
look~~~~~~~~~~~~~~~~th~~~~~~~~~~
~~e fire
will~~~~~~~~~~~~~~~~~~~ eyes
forewa~~~~~~~~~~~~~.

Damaged and unreadable section of The Grim Knot

CHAPTER 22

Death at One's Side

MY LIFE FLASHED BEFORE my eyes. I could see Francine holding me tight after I had fallen out of our second-story apartment window when I was nine. I could see her funeral, and Mr. Claude telling me I was being shipped off to Kingsplot. I could see Millie pretending to care, and my father, who I'd believed was my uncle, telling me how he had been wrong to only watch the skies when so much was happening all around him. I could see Kate's face as she realized I thought she was one of the bad guys.

Most important, out of the corner of my right eye I could see Pip dropping debris onto Ishmael and Ishmael jerking his head up to roar at Pip. The portable light Pip had taken from the courtyard bounced off Ishmael and crashed on the ground. Ishmael flexed his legs and rocketed into the sky toward Pip.

The two huge dragons collided in midair. It sounded like two wet stones scraping against one another.

Ishmael began to tear at Pip with his back talons. The great white dragon blew flames from his mouth. The wet gray sky came alive in a shower of fireworks.

In the sky, Ishmael flapped his wings and bit at Pip's neck. Pip wailed as Ishmael threw her toward the ground. Pip dropped like a stone, but she opened her wings and caught herself before hitting the ground.

With a final roar, Ishmael flew away to continue doing what he was destined to do.

I looked at Wyatt, standing directly above me. He was breathing hard and his face was whiter than Ishmael.

"Are you okay?" he asked, reaching out to help me up.

I wiped dragon drool from my eyes and nodded my head.

We both looked at Pip.

"Why did it save you?"

"I'm not sure," I said. "I think the dragons are more confused than they should be."

The poor dragon was twenty feet away from us, shaking her head. She flapped her wings and blew a weak stream of smoke from her nostrils. She looked fearsome but tired. She looked at me and blinked.

"Is it going to eat us?" Wyatt whispered, handing me the black staff.

"I don't think so," I whispered back, but holding the stick in front of me just in case.

Pip looked away. She raised her head and stepped sideways over to a metal bench. With one talon, she pulled the bench out of the ground and then turned to reach for more worthless spoil. Her wide hairy back was facing us.

"I'm going to need a ride to the manor," I said to Wyatt.

"What does that mean?" he asked, concerned.

"I've got to find Aeron and end this. Get the police up to the manor as fast as possible," I ordered.

"But how are—"

I didn't wait around to hear the rest of his question. I ran toward Pip and climbed up her back, still holding onto the staff.

"You're crazy!" Wyatt yelled.

"You're probably right," I yelled back.

And with that, Pip and I were off.

Morgan Phillips was a selfish man. Like his ancestor Edward, he cared only for money and power. After Morgan returned to America from Europe, he married a woman named Anne. They had one daughter and one son. Their son's name was Aeron. Seduced by the possibility of untold wealth, Morgan woke one of the stones. The single dragon devoured him and then died.

Excerpt from section twelve of The Grim Knot, *as recorded by Aeron Phillips*

CHAPTER 23

I Know It's Ending

WE RACED THROUGH THE GRAY AIR, hugging the slopes of the mountain and flying just above the height of the trees. We popped into the clouds and skimmed over the smaller mountains. Pip flew through the short tunnel. The darkness made my thoughts less jumbled and made the whole day feel like a dream.

I shook my head.

As we popped out of the tunnel, I could see the manor through the clouds. We flew past the manor and back toward the conservatory.

Pip screamed as she descended through the mist and into the conservatory. The entire conservatory was filled with all kinds of torn-up pieces of buildings and objects. Pip dropped everything she had pillaged and then settled onto a large heap of twisted metal and broken wood.

I slid off Pip's back, holding the black staff tightly in my right hand. I climbed down a bronze statue of a small child that had once stood in front of the hospital.

Pip moaned and I turned to look at her. She wobbled, leaning over as she tried to step forward. She fell to the ground in a cloud of debris and dirt.

"Pip," I whispered.

The dragon had been through enough. The fight with Ishmael had made her even weaker. I stepped up to the poor beast and stretched my left hand out to touch Pip above her right eye.

She snorted weakly.

"I'm sorry," I said, feeling as if my throat was filled with mud. I thought about everyone in my family history who had selfishly used these amazing creatures to get gain and felt the mud turn to stone in my throat.

Pip exhaled and small streams of fire dripped from her mouth like lava.

I patted Pip again and could feel her head dissolving beneath my touch. As Pip disappeared, the wind lifted the bits up, making it look like the corners of her mouth were smiling.

"Sorry," I said again.

A strong fist of wind punched through the conservatory

and finished Pip off. I wanted to take a minute to mourn, but I could hear my name being called.

"Hello?" I asked, looking around.

I could barely see past the stuff the dragons had pillaged and dropped off. I stepped over another pile of junk and listened.

Someone *was* calling my name.

I looked around for a few seconds before I realized the sound was coming from below me. I looked down, but couldn't see anything but junk.

"Down here," Kate's muffled voice yelled.

The fading light made it hard to see. I climbed carefully over a small car, a trampoline, and another metal statue. I was able to slide down the back of a metal street sign, landing next to the shack. The door to the shack was permanently pinned open by a couple dozen sets of golf clubs.

The metal grate was gone, so I easily hopped down the hole. Before my feet had even hit the floor I could hear Kate yelling.

"Beck! Over here."

I ran down the tunnel to the metal gate and bars. The cage was dark, covered with all the pillaged items in the conservatory above. As my eyes adjusted I could see Kate and Scott. I was really only happy to see Kate. She looked pretty worried though—emphasis on *pretty*.

"Who locked you up?" I asked. "Why did Thomas lock Scott in there with you?"

"It wasn't Thomas," Kate said. "It was Milo. Thomas and the others are locked up in the stables."

"Why?" I asked, confused.

"Milo's been impersonating everyone," Scott said. "After Thomas and Millie locked you in your room for safety that night, Milo took your form and lured all of them into the stables. They didn't know how you got out, but Milo was so adamant that they follow."

"So it wasn't Thomas who boarded up my windows?" I said, looking at Scott.

He shook his head.

"They didn't bring me to Kingsplot just to wake the dragons?"

"Nonsense," Scott insisted. "Millie and Wane? Come now. They were so happy to hear you were coming. We didn't even tell Aeron because we knew he'd say no. Of course, our one reservation was about the stories we've heard forever. And look what happened."

I still didn't completely trust Scott.

"I was told Thomas and Millie sent for me."

"They got a call from a gentleman telling us who to contact," Scott said.

"Must have been Milo," Kate deduced.

"I'm so sorry, Beck," Scott said. "I know I've been harsh, but it was out of concern for you. We would never hurt you, you know that."

I knew Kate was trapped in a rusted, underground cage beneath piles of wreckage pillaged from Kingsplot. I knew Milo was out there somewhere. I didn't know where Aeron was. Despite what I did or didn't know, I felt a great sense of relief knowing that Millie and Thomas and Wane had not betrayed me.

"Thomas said you needed money for taxes," I argued.

"That wasn't Thomas," Scott said. "We still have another whole floor of furniture to sell. Plus there's plenty of land we could sell off. Milo was lying to you."

"So how'd you get in here?" I asked Kate.

"Thanks to you," she said. "Milo took your form. I thought I was following you down here. I should have been suspicious, considering some of the nice things you were saying."

It might have been my imagination, but it looked like Kate was blushing a little.

"Wow, Milo's good," I said.

"After he locked me up, he found Scott," Kate said.

"He wants the entire Pillage fortune," Scott said. "He feels it belongs to him."

"It was his curse that started it," I growled, trying to pop the door open on the cage. I shook my head. "It won't budge."

"Just go," Kate said, stepping as close to the bars as she could. "Stop him."

I knew what I needed to do, but there was something inside of me causing me to pause.

"Go!" Kate insisted. "What are you waiting for?"

I leaned in and kissed her. I had never kissed anyone before. In fact, I couldn't remember if I had even ever kissed my mother. I don't know what I was expecting, but what it felt like was a great surprise. I had fallen from vents, scaled buildings, and flown on the backs of dragons, yet somehow all of those things seemed a bit less amazing now. I banged the side of my head on the bars as I pulled back.

"Ow," I said.

"What was that?" Kate said breathlessly.

Scott politely turned away.

"I figured if I could kill a dragon, I could kiss a girl."

"You are so strange," she whispered kindly.

"I feel the same about you," I said, smiling. "I'll be back as soon as possible."

I made my way back up the hole and into the conservatory. The oncoming night covered the dragon's junk in lumpy shadows. I climbed to the top of a pile and looked down, surprised to see Aeron moving toward me. He was working through a tangle of metal.

I scrambled toward him.

"Are you okay?" I asked.

"I couldn't stop him," Aeron admitted. "Milo's going to the manor. He said you were hurt."

Aeron balanced himself on a large piece of roof. We were in the middle of the conservatory, surrounded by everything the dragons had brought back. Aeron looked around.

"Kingsplot must be a mess," he commented unnecessarily.

"Half of it's here," I said. "Although I don't really see anything of value."

"I think you're wrong," Aeron said. "This conservatory is fat with gain. Milo will make a fortune."

"What?" I asked.

"It's fat with gain. There's a fortune here."

I could hear Ishmael screaming in the distance as he made another approach. Something didn't feel right.

"How many dragons are left?" Aeron asked.

"Two or three," I lied, looking closely at him.

"Good." Aeron relaxed.

"Do you know where everyone else is?" I questioned.

"Hiding in the manor, I think."

"Excellent."

The mist-filled clouds stretched just a bit, exposing the early-night sky. I could see Ishmael's dark shadow swoop over the side of the conservatory as he turned to come in for a landing. The sound of his wings flapping in the air matched the beating of my racing heart.

"What do we do now?" I asked.

"We should wait here," he said, stepping closer.

"Why?"

"As the dragons return, we can pick them off," he answered.

I looked at the staff in my hand, knowing that it would be of no use on the last dragon. I hefted it in my hand.

"Here you go, Aeron," I said loudly. "You'll need this."

Ishmael was behind Aeron, heading toward us. I tossed the staff to him just as Ishmael dropped into the conservatory. I could see his blue eyes recognize Aeron. In one smooth motion, Ishmael opened his jaws, releasing the metal trash bin he carried, and then, exposing a second and a third row of teeth, he turned his head sideways.

Aeron spun around to look at him as the dragon closed his jaws, consuming him completely with one bite.

It was frightening to watch.

Ishmael shot straight up into the air with Aeron in his mouth.

"I hope I'm right," I whispered.

I watched Ishmael rise higher and higher.

"'Fat with gain'?" I said to myself. "Who talks like that?"

Ishmael became a winged dot in the distance and then, suddenly, he began to drop down. I could see his wings fold in as he fell, back first, to the ground. I held my hand up to my eyes, watching him plummet toward earth. He began to break up, bits of him trailing behind him like a comet in the moonlight.

Just as I was about to run for cover, Ishmael burst apart, every bit of him shooting off into a thousand directions like a snowy firework.

Ishmael was gone.

Milo was gone.

The curse was broken.

A single stone dropped from the sky and pounded the ground two feet in front of me.

I felt like swearing. Instead, I picked up the rock and looked closely at it. It was heavy, but not as heavy as the ones I had planted. It looked like a normal, round rock. When I touched it, the center glowed slightly, but when I set it down, nothing happened. I picked it back up and scaled the ivy out of the conservatory. The climb out wasn't nearly as long, seeing as how the conservatory was two-thirds filled with junk.

I dropped outside the wall and ran through the woods, my heart and throat competing over which could hurt worse. I slowed, weaving between trees and undergrowth until I reached the rock pasture. I stared at the millions and millions of rocks as I held the single stone in my hand.

I tightened my fingers around the rock.

"No Pillage has ever had the courage to give up the stones," Aeron said, stepping out from behind the trees. His breath was labored and his face gray.

"I read that," I said quietly, not entirely surprised to see him.

"Not even me," Aeron admitted. "I couldn't simply get rid of them. So I had to remove myself."

"How'd you find me?" I asked.

"I saw you climb from the conservatory," he explained. "I released Thomas and Millie and Wane from the stables. I must say they were pretty surprised to see me. I was coming for Milo when I saw you on the ivy."

"Milo's dead," I said. "He impersonated the wrong person. I guess the dragon recognized the Pillage features."

Aeron smiled, putting his hand on my shoulder. "Brilliant."

"Unless I was wrong," I said, suddenly concerned. "How do *you* feel about all of that treasure the dragons brought back?"

"That useless junk?" he questioned with a smile.

I sighed with relief.

Aeron looked at the rock in my hand.

"The final dragon left this," I said, holding it up.

Aeron reached out, but then pulled his hands back, looking guilty.

I stared out over the stone field. It was almost dark.

I didn't want to be like Edward or Bruno. I had read their mistakes in *The Grim Knot,* and I wanted no part of it. Sure there was a bit of me that wished I could fly around on a dragon's back, scooping up gold and silver, but that bit was buried by a desire to be more like my other ancestor Hermitage, or my father, Aeron. The chain had to be broken.

"Turn around," I whispered, standing with my back to the rock field.

"What?" my father asked.

"Turn around."

Aeron looked proud. He slowly turned around next to me.

I threw the rock over my shoulder as far as I could. I could hear the rock crack and bounce against other stones as it landed.

Neither one of us glanced back.

The sound of sirens could faintly be heard coming from the direction of the mansion.

"I had one of my friends bring the police," I informed Aeron. "I wasn't sure if we'd need the help."

"I guess you underestimated yourself," he smiled.

The sirens were growing louder.

"They can help us bust out Kate and Scott," I suggested. "You know, we're going to have some major explaining to do to the people of Kingsplot."

"The truth might be hard to swallow at times, but there is satisfaction in the digestion."

I stared at Aeron.

"I mean the truth will prevail," he clarified.

I shook my head, embarrassed for adults everywhere.

Aeron smiled as we walked through the dark forest toward the sound of sirens.

"So is this the end?" I asked.

"I suppose," Aeron said. "Although it feels a bit like a beginning."

I completely agreed.

Aeron married a woman named Laurel. She died giving birth to their only child, a boy named Beck. Aeron went temporarily mad with grief. His sister, Francine, took Beck away, with the promise of never returning. Fortunately, for everyone everywhere, some promises are made to be broken.

CHAPTER 24

Having Everything Now

THERE WAS SO MUCH FOOD. Millie felt awful about me ever believing that she could have been cruel—so awful she was now trying to kill me with biscuits and gravy. My stomach complained as I stood in the kitchen eating a plate full of buttery cakes and warm roast, leaning against the counter. Thomas and Wane were in the kitchen also. Millie kept looking up from what she was doing and winking at me with her one straight eye.

"Is it okay?" she asked for the third time.

"Sublime," I said, using another of my newly learned words.

"He might need more juice," Thomas said, reaching for the half-full glass in front of me.

"I'll get him some," Wane insisted.

"Seriously," I smiled. "I'm fine."

All three smiled back.

Kingsplot and Callowbrow were far from put back together. There were still entire buildings that needed to be rebuilt or repaired and large holes remained everywhere. At Callowbrow, we were holding most of our classes in portables that the school had brought in and set up in the parking lot. Most of the damage in Kingsplot had been in the center of town. And even though eighty-seven people were injured, nobody had been killed. A woman who had been picked up and dropped off in the conservatory was planning to write a book about her experiences.

It had taken a lot of explaining to get the cops to understand what had happened. If they had not seen for themselves the dragons tearing apart the town, they would have never believed us. Videos of the dragons had been showing up on TV and the Internet. In fact, our small, sleepy town had been inundated with thousands and thousands of curious tourists.

A blowtorch had been necessary to get Kate and Scott out of the cage. Kate had seen Milo with a key, but Milo was no longer around. Aeron speculated it was the key Taft had sent with his son, Morgan, to his wife, Esmeralda in Europe. Milo must have followed Morgan and discovered the truth about where the Pillage family had gone.

Aeron also wondered if Milo had even been following me,

trying to influence Francine. I figured he had taken the form of one of the two passengers who had ridden the train into town with me. He had been a masterful magician who could work trick candles and impersonations, but he couldn't boss around the foliage or hatch a dragon egg like a Pillage. For that, he had needed Aeron or me. Luckily for all of us, Milo was finally gone.

Aeron was slowly adjusting to being slightly normal. So much of the insanity that Thomas and Millie and Wane had seen in him in the last few years had actually been Milo's doing. We figured Milo had taken on our shapes and had multiple conversations with each of us at different points in time, trying to get us to do what he wanted.

Aeron decided to sell off some of our land to cover the costs of helping to repair Kingsplot. With any luck, we would be able to keep the manor. I didn't really care. Even if my father had to sell the manor, at least we would be together. I missed Francine, but I knew she would always be with me. It was interesting how much sense her journal now made with the new knowledge I had of the family we both came from.

Aeron was trying hard to adjust to life below the seventh floor. He still slept in the dome, but was making his way down more often. He was also trying to figure out how to be a dad. It was sort of nice that we both had to figure things out together.

Scott came through the kitchen door.

"Look what I found outside," he said.

Kate walked in behind him. She waved at everyone and stepped up next to me.

"Things are looking nice around here," she said, commenting on all the cleanup and removal that was happening. "It almost looks like the way it was."

"Almost," Millie smiled. "But we didn't have such pretty visitors before."

Scott was about to say, "Thank you," but stopped. "Oh, you mean the girl."

It was the first joke I had ever seen him attempt. It wasn't too bad, considering how awful adult senses of humor can be.

"Wyatt gave me this," Kate said, handing me a note. "He tried to find you at school."

I read the note out loud, "Tomorrow. After school. In the park."

"Everything okay?" Kate asked.

"Yeah, we're playing basketball tomorrow," I answered. "You in?"

"Of course." Kate smiled, turning to make sure I would see it.

"You'll need some snacks," Millie said anxiously. "I'd better get started. Maybe some cookies, or pretzels."

Before I could protest, a new shadow darkened the door—

Aeron. He looked more nervous than when he had been fighting dragons. He cleared his throat.

"I just thought I'd come down and see what's going on," he said awkwardly. It was obvious he had tried to comb his hair that morning. He was also wearing semi-normal clothes and had trimmed his beard.

We all looked at each other, still not completely sure how to handle him just popping in.

"We were about to make cookies," I said happily. "You're welcome to help. Millie's recipe is easy."

He looked at everyone's faces, then shook his head in disbelief. "Aeron and Beck Phillips making cookies," he laughed.

"Beck *Pillage*," I corrected.

My dad liked that.

Kate squeezed my hand. Then she opened the cupboard, looking for sugar as I reached for the mixing bowls.